Sabine  doctor's cab
she steps o
corridor tha
wears white
her thighs.

When she .... Doctor Gordon's door, he opens it immediately.

"You're late."

She makes Doctor Gordon crawl to her. There's no need to say anything because it's been done before and he knows the doing of it. He's sweating now, the sweat showing on his high pink forehead as he crawls over the floor with his eyes on Sabine's legs.

Finally he arrives. He kisses her legs. Sabine sits motionless as Doctor Gordon runs his lips over the silk of her stockings.

"I want your help," she says.

"My help?"

"There's a passenger named Fernando Jimenez. He's a diplomat, I think. I want you to find out everything you can about him and then tell me what you learn. Will you do that, darling?"

"Fernando Jimenez."

"Yes, that's it."

"All right."

"You're sweet."

She opens her thighs to his face. Does he murmur something? Sabine shudders as his tongue begins tickling the insides of her thighs.

Also Published by BLUE MOON BOOKS

SABINE

David Vian

BLUE MOON BOOKS, INC. NEW YORK

Sabine
ISBN 0-8216-5029-7
CIP data available from Library of Congress

Manufactured in the United States of America
Published by Blue Moon Books, Inc.
61 Fourth Avenue
New York, NY 10003

Cover design by Steve Brower

Chapter One

*

Two days out of Valparaiso: April 17, 1936

From here the sky is so sad. From here there is nothing but the open sky, the bowl of the sky above the ocean a vast blue emptiness, an endless blue world. We see only a single cloud, a small white cloud shaped like a breast, the nipple of the breast pointing to the zenith, a nipple so turgid it begs for the lips.

Sabine looks at the ocean, the cloud, the sky, the endless blue. She sits in a deck chair with a glass of lemonade in her left hand.

The deck of the ship dazzles the eyes, the white, the boards, the white posts, the gleaming white enamel on the stacks, the white funnels.

Over there people strolling along the rail: two passengers with linked arms. Italians? They both wear white clothes. The man is decently dressed. The woman is completely out of fashion, as thin as a stick and her dress too long. She wears a cloche hat but the style no longer suits her.

The breeze changes. First it appears, then dallies, then vanishes again. Always blowing from the west. Sabine think it's the west. She's an awful sailor, completely ignorant. This morning Leon laughed at her ignorance and she had to warn him.

And where is Santiago? Over there, somewhere beyond the horizon. Santiago, Santiago;

goodbye, Santiago. Goodbye to the Mapocho and the Santa Lucia and the Alameda de las Delicias. Oh dear yes, the Alameda de las Delicias. Sabine muses. Cherie, your mind is twisted in its memories. One should not sit facing the land when one is leaving it.

She decides to adjust her fichu to hide her breasts. That Roman bitch will frown. The husband will smile and the bitch will frown. A thin frown gurgling out of the mud of the Tiber. And in any case Sabine does not want the sun there. The skin between the breasts should be milk-white, like the white of the deck, the purest of whites.

That portrait painter in Vina del Mar with the white paint on his nose. Zinc white, he said. Sabine, this is the purest of zinc-white. Well, he wasn't that charming, was he?

Now she thinks of Leon again. Leon has a passion for silk. Silk drawers. Silk stockings. He adores her silk stockings. The garters. The ribbons. His tongue licking along the ribbons. Sabine amuses herself thinking of Leon's tongue. And now the Roman bitch is here and the man of course is smiling at Sabine with another glance at her ankles. Yes, my sweet, you may kiss my foot. Sabine would have him grovelling while the Roman bitch screams with jealousy.

Is it easy? No, it is not easy. Not simple. Nothing is simple in this life.

Sabine likes the name of this ship. Reina del Pacifico. The Queen. Yes, she likes the name.

Away now, the Italians are away and once again Sabine sits here alone.

Leon, will you really abandon me?

Sabine considers it, then she tells herself that truly if Leon dies he will certainly not be there for her.

But of course she'll have something more than memories.

She thinks of Leon's face. Last evening before dinner he was on his knees with that red flush in his face. What an absurd time to speak to her of calamities. One does not want calamities at a quarter to eight in the evening. First he cajoles her into lifting her dress to have a sniff at her and then he speaks to her of calamities.

She wanted to kick him.

Cherie, you must think.

Is the captain handsome? Sabine thought she would see the captain at dinner last evening, but his table was empty. Isn't that strange? One expects things.

Leon does adore Sabine's white hat. "Sabine, I adore you." He mumbles at her while his face tickles the insides of her thighs above her silk stockings.

Now one of the waiters arrives with a silver tray in his hand. Sabine orders a coffee and when the coffee is brought to her she tips the waiter. Sabine notices the waiter looks tired and she wonders if he has a girl somewhere. Is he Chilean? From Santiago? A girl in Santiago? Sabine tells herself that Santiago was indeed lovely and she did have a lovely time with Leon, all those lovely hours on the boulevards and the parties in the cool evenings and her secret amusements when she was in the mood for them.

Dark-eyed boys near the cathedral. Darling, don't think of that now. You mustn't think of it because it's all gone and the weather is much too hot for it.

She does want to see Paris again.

She will not think of calamities.

*

In their cabin, Leon smiles at Sabine.

"Did you enjoy the deck?"

"Yes, I liked it. You ought to get some sun."

"In the afternoon, I suppose."

"Leon, you must tell me the truth about that business."

"Darling, what business?"

"Your illness."

Leon turns away.

"I'm reaching the end."

"You're still young."

"Don't be silly, I'm past sixty."

"You must tell me about it. I mean about your illness."

"My dear, it's the heart. They don't last, you know. One can't go on forever, can one?"

"That's absurd."

"Absurd?"

"I don't like this game."

"But it's not a game."

"Leon, I refuse to accept it. You know how annoyed I become."

"Yes, I do know."

"You're as healthy as a young man."

"I'm afraid I'll die before we reach Cherbourg."

"No."

"Yes, my darling."

"Oh Leon."

"Certainly before we reach Cherbourg."

"I refuse to believe it. I won't leave this cabin until you tell me that it's not true."

"Darling, you must believe me. And we must go on as always. You're a young woman and you must go on. It's almost time for lunch now and I want you with me."

"I'll change my clothes. I'll wear black."

Leon groans.

"Sabine, please . . ."

"Well, I'll change my clothes just the same."

He sits and watches her as she undresses. He sits there with his eyes so bright and his fingers pulling at his chin. Can he possibly be at death's door? Sabine is uneasy. What does she know about such things? When he sees her in her chemise, he reaches out to touch her hip.

Sabine frowns.

"You seem healthy enough for that."

Leon chuckles.

"Yes."

Everything off now. She stands there wearing nothing but her white stockings and her white slippers. She does like white. Leon's eyes are fixed on her belly, on her thicket. She moves closer to where he sits and she holds one of her breasts to his mouth.

"Suck this one."

He sucks. His lips wet and clinging. His nose tickling her breast.

"Leon, tell me it's not true."

His lips make a smacking sound as they pull away from her nipple.

"But it is."

"The doctors in Santiago are fools."

"I haven't seen any doctors."

"My God."

"Darling, a doctor isn't necessary. I'll be dead before Cherbourg and nothing will stop it."

He continues sucking her breasts. She feeds him. First the right and then the left. Her nipples are like hard pebbles, dark pebbles glistening now as Leon's lips glisten.

Oh yes.

Sabine shudders.

She hides the shuddering. It's never any good to let them see the shuddering. She watches his mouth. She feels the quivering in her sex, the hot tingling, the lovely heat of it.

She pushes him away.

"That's enough, Leon. If I'm to dress for lunch, I need to get on with it."

*

A noisy crowd in the dining room. Mostly Chileans, Sabine thinks. All these Italians speaking Spanish. Or they might be Spaniards speaking Spanish. Joking with the waiters about the menu.

Sabine and Leon have fish and white wine. Leon eats his food with gusto and Sabine refuses to accept the notion that he's dying.

She has an aversion to the midday meal on this ship. Something for the Germans. Are the Germans at it again? And here in this dining room ten thousand miles around the underside of the world. Those Teutonic faces in the corner near that ugly plant. That German jeweler in Valaparaiso?

Now she sees the captain of the ship. His lovely white uniform. An Englishman with pink cheeks and a red moustache, smiling as he bows to his passengers. Sabine considers the captain. With the English the moustache is a deception. They rarely know what to do with it; they rarely know how to tickle with it. Still, the red moustache is intriguing. The captain might be knowledgeable. If he knows how to maneuver his ship he might know how to maneuver his moustache. Sabine thinks about the captain of the Reina del Pacifico tickling her gigi with his red moustache. Fore and aft, dear captain; fore and aft.

Leon talks with equanimity about his impending death.

"One must be philosophical."

"Leon, I will not allow this game to continue. I'll punish you for it."

"Sabine, please . . ."

"You're not serious."

"I'm quite serious. One is always serious about one's own death."

His mouth is distracting. All the amusements crowd Sabine's mind. Leon's mouth in the cabin less than an hour ago.

And the eyes of the men. She has the eyes of the men on her. Their imaginings. That one with his defiant chin so eager to nestle against her proclivities.

All the women in the room seem to be talking

at once, fingers waving like tentacles, their red lips continually opening, closing, opening again.

"Sabine, you've hardly touched your fish."

"I'm thinking."

*

The ship's doctor is a young Englishman with hair the color of sand and eyes the color of a pale blue sky. The eyes gaze at Sabine, at her face, at her breasts, at the flesh of her arms.

Sabine nods at the English doctor.

"I'm here concerning Monsieur Mabeuf. Monsieur Leon Mabeuf."

"Your husband, madam?"

"My benefactor."

"I see."

See what? What is it that he sees?

"Are you the doctor?"

"Yes, madam. And what seems to be the trouble with Monsieur Mabeuf?"

"He talks about dying. He seems to think he's going to die very soon. Is that possible?"

The doctor shrugs. An English shrug.

"Is Monsieur Mabeuf ill?"

"I don't know. I don't think so."

The air in the infirmary has a sweet smell. Is it ether? Yes of course. Even on a ship one must have the smell of it. Sabine quivers. She hates hospitals.

The doctor's eyes are on Sabine's breasts again and Sabine imagines his brain in a fever as he thinks of his nose against her skin.

"Tell me about Monsieur Mabeuf," the doctor says.

"He's a man of sixty and he's quite rational."

"I see."

He sees again.

"Doctor, what do you think?"

"I suppose I ought to examine him. I'll go to his cabin if you like."

*

Sabine waits in the ship's salon. She sits alone and she thinks about Leon and the doctor. She imagines herself in the doctor's infirmary again. But now he's to examine Sabine and not Leon. He points at the white screen in the corner and he asks Sabine to remove her clothes. Does he watch her as she walks across the room? Behind the screen, Sabine feels an excitement as she undresses. She touches the points of her nipples. She thinks about the English doctor. She wants the truth about Leon. The ship is rolling now and Sabine finds the movement pleasant. She finishes undressing but she leaves her stockings on. She walks away from the screen wearing her stockings and slippers and as soon as the doctor sees her the pink color of his face becomes darker. Sabine walks towards him like a naughty postcard come to life. Yes, the English doctor is blushing. And he has a superb erection. When Sabine finally stands before him, she can see the dimensions in his trousers. She fixes her eyes on the twitching of his penis.

"Do show it to me," Sabine says.

The doctor groans. He glances at the door.

"Dear God . . ."

He stands paralyzed. Then finally he yields. He

brings his penis out. The knob is only half exposed.

Sabine tells him to pull the hood back.

"You want to show the knob a bit more."

The doctor's eyes are glazed. Sabine stares calmly at the wet tip of his organ. He groans. She watches as he curls his fingers around the column of swollen flesh. The doctor trembles. He shows a madness in his eyes. His fingers begin moving. Sabine watches it carefully. She watches until he groans again, until the pearls begin flying.

A shudder passes through Sabine as she sits there in the salon and thinks about the English doctor's organ spurting so lavishly in his infirmary.

The doctor reminds her more of a priest than a doctor. Sabine adores priests who are chaste. Is the English doctor chaste? She thinks of priests in the shadowed corners of cathedrals. Their flesh is so white under the dark cloth. She imagines them throbbing in their devotions. Some of the younger ones have such an innocence in the eyes. They keep their eyes lowered in the presence of women. And afterward, in a corner with a smell of incense, they touch themselves as they contemplate their transgressions.

Now Sabine thinks of her last confession: an impulse in Santiago. She happened to visit the cathedral while the choir was singing and she was suddenly overcome with a religious fervor. Was it the memory of her mother? Sabine remembers her mother's devotions. As a girl Sabine often thought of nuns and convents and the secrets of religious ecstasies. The whisperings of her girlfriends. The images of bleeding hands. Oh yes, the secrets. Sometimes she imagined she could hear the moaning of the nuns when she passed the convent on her way home from school.

As a child Sabine was very timid and afraid of dark rooms. Her father often teased her about her fears, teasing her at the dinner table, teasing her in the presence of her aunts.

Sabine hated the old house where she spent her childhood. She often had fantasies that the house had suddenly become transformed into something else. She imagined herself returning from school, turning that last cornèr to find that her house had become a castle. She adored reading stories about castles and kings and the luxuries of the king's daughters. She liked games in isolation and her mother would scold her for it. "You dream too much," her mother said. Sabine continued dreaming. That was certainly one activity they could not prevent. They might forbid it but they could not prevent it.

Dreaming of a prince. What a laugh. Sabine squirms now as she thinks of it. How amusing it is the way the mind paints color into the grey of the past. She has memories of cold days with her parents. And then the war came and the old house that was not a castle was destroyed. All that mud in March. Sabine thinks of herself as a child. Did that child actually exist? Sabine begins to cry now. She feels the tears in her eyes and she strains to hold them back. What an annoyance to cry like this in a public place while one is sitting alone. You're a child, she thinks. What you need is a bosom to cry upon, a warm bosom to console you. Yes, why not? Sabine has a fondness for feminine comforts. Her eyes are always attracted by a pair of full breasts. She imagines them as pillows, and then she imagines them as objects of pleasure. She likes to think of full breasts with extended nipples. Dark nipples like the nipples of her mother. Sabine's own breasts are full and round and thickly pointed. Sabine adores sucking at a breast. She understands the hunger of men for it. Sabine has known the hunger herself, the hunger and the satiation, the tangle of female flesh in a warm bed.

Don't be absurd, Sabine thinks.

But she hates hypocrisy. All these women who give the appearance of stuffed birds. And then the parade is over and in secret corners the fingers are sliding over their smooth bellies to find their pleasures. The eyes turn in their moanings, their nipples extended as they reach each secret crisis.

Sabine cries often, and often she has no idea why.

Is it true that her parents coddled and pampered her and that her memories of them are false?

As a schoolchild she was always absent-minded, always staring in front of her and thinking about everything except her schoolwork.

The path of her life is a labyrinth and she sees no way out of it.

*

The doctor has just examined Leon and now he comes out of the cabin to talk to Sabine at the rail.

"Madame Mabeuf . . ."

"I am not Madame Mabeuf. My name is Sabine Boulanger."

"Miss Boulanger."

"Tell me about Monsieur Mabeuf."

"I can't find anything wrong with him."

"What do you mean?"

The doctor shakes his head.

"I'm afraid there isn't anything I can do."

"Then he'll die?"

"One can't predict these things . . ."

"But he's convinced he's dying."

"He needs a bit of fresh air. I suppose this voyage will give him enough of that."

*

"Leon, you ought to have told me."

"But I did."

"You ought to have told me in Santiago. I was careless not to listen to you. It's horrible how careless I've been."

"No, you're not careless."

"But you're convinced you're going to die."

"Yes, I'm afraid so."

"How long do you think?"

"Before we reach Cherbourg."

"My God."

"Sabine, darling . . ."

"I won't travel any more. I'll have an apartment in Paris and I won't go anywhere. Not without my Leon."

"You're sweet."

"Leon, how much is there? How much will I have?"

"Sabine, I must tell you . . ."

"An apartment and enough to live comfortably, I should think. You might consider giving something to that niece of yours. I don't like her but I suppose she ought to have something."

"Sabine, I must tell you there isn't anything."

"But not any of the other relatives. That crowd in Dijon. The way they snubbed me at your brother's funeral."

"There isn't anything."

"No one but your niece, Leon."

"Sabine, there isn't anything."

"There isn't anything of what?"

"There isn't anything, Sabine. The accounts are empty, everything gone. There isn't anything for anyone."

Chapter Two

*

Two years before in Paris, Sabine is in the apartment of Amelie Vedel at five o'clock in the afternoon. The two women lounge in Amelie's bedroom, lulled into serenity by the open windows, the warm air, the noise of the Boulevard Haussmann.

Once again Amelie reminds Sabine of the imminent arrival of Amelie's lover.

"But you mustn't leave."

"It's time for me to go."

"No, I want you to meet him."

The lover's name is Claude Orac, and although Amelie has been his mistress for nearly three months, Sabine has never had a look at him.

Sabine agrees to stay.

Ten minutes pass and finally Amelie's lover arrives. But he's not alone. Claude Orac comes with a friend and the friend is introduced to the women as Leon Mabeuf.

Monsieur Mabeuf is a man of middling size, a healthy color in his cheeks and hardly any grey in his hair.

The four of them sit and talk and Sabine is soon aware that Mabeuf has his eyes on her.

And in Mabeuf's eyes there is everything.

Sabine can always tell by the eyes. All the strengths and weaknesses are evident in the eyes, the hopes, the longing, the fire of hidden passions. One can see it in both men and women, the need for something.

As Sabine returns his glance, Mabeuf is blushing, merely a faint increase in the pink of his cheeks, but blushing nevertheless. Blushing in his face and blushing in his eyes.

Mabeuf is aware of Sabine's understanding now. He's like a small boy who suddenly becomes aware that his schoolmistress knows all his tricks.

Does Sabine want him? She considers the question. She requires certain comforts and certainly men like Mabeuf can provide them. She has no one at the moment, nothing but a packet of soiled letters from an aging lover who seems lost in Indochina. Yes, Mabeuf might be interesting.

Sabine's instinct tells her to proceed carefully. One must accept the advantage of instinct. Mabeuf is not to be had by clumsy force; a degree of subtlety is required and the amusement is therefore enhanced.

She teases him with her legs, her silk-covered ankles, her foot turning, twisting, pulling at his eyes, forcing him to think of her body.

She wonders about Mabeuf's tendencies. Is it his pleasure to grovel? She does not like grovelling men. A man of substance should not grovel in the dust. Kiss the foot, perhaps, but not grovel in the dust.

They must be cultivated. A man like Mabeuf has to be stroked into his own understanding.

His eyes are always upon her. The four of them talk of the latest amusements in Paris, the new music in the clubs, the new aeroplanes that can be seen on the tarmac at Le Bourget, but Mabeuf's eyes never waver from Sabine's legs.

Sabine is certain Mabeuf is in a state of arousal. He sits hunched forward a bit as if to hide the presence of his erection.

Sabine decides her clothes are perfect for the occasion, a happy coincidence, an ensemble perfect for the likes of Mabeuf. She knows his inclinations. He's a man who likes a woman to be carefully tailored. Sabine wears a light brown linen suit with a long jacket, a pleated skirt and brown snakeskin shoes and beige silk stockings. Mabeuf's eyes keep returning to Sabine's shoes. Is it the snakeskin leather or the pointed heels? She sits with her legs crossed, her right ankle turning under Mabeuf's attentive eyes.

Now Sabine notices that Amelie is amused. Amelie is too astute not to recognize what is happening, too much the Parisian woman not to understand completely.

But Amelie soon turns her attention away. Amelie and her lover ignore Sabine and Mabeuf. Sabine has Mabeuf to herself, his eyes, his complete attention, his hunger burning in his face.

She commands him with her eyes, a silent commanding, an imposition of the will, an electric arc of understanding between them.

Sabine sips her wine, gazes at Mabeuf, the wet of the wine on her lips as she looks at him.

All of them rise when it's time for the men to leave. Mabeuf leans forward to kiss Sabine's hand, his lips tickling her fingers, his eyes half closed as he savors the moment.

When the men are gone, Amelie laughs at

Sabine.

"He's rich but he has someone."

"He's quaint."

"Darling, he's a puppy."

"How rich?"

"It's mines, I think. Mining in South America."

"South America? Oh dear."

"You won't get him."

"I don't know."

Amelie laughs again.

"Poor fellow."

But for Sabine it's more than the mere challenge. She needs Mabeuf. She needs the comforts.

*

Within a week Sabine receives a short letter from Leon Mabeuf.

A flowery hand expresses his admiration. Would she be willing to meet him somewhere? He names a place and a time and he writes he would be deeply happy at her arrival.

And so a few days later in the afternoon, Sabine has a rendezvous with Leon Mabeuf near the Rue de Madrid.

Rain has been falling all day and they sit indoors. The café is crowded, the usual late afternoon rush before the place becomes dismal in the early evening.

Mabeuf seems thankful that he and Sabine are ignored by the busy waiters. After the first service of cake and cognac, Mabeuf fixes his complete attention on Sabine.

"I'm so happy you're here," he says.

Sabine looks at the crowd. She doesn't mind it.

Five o'clock is the most interesting hour to be in a café of this sort.

They talk of trivialities, the weather, the horse races, the rumblings in Europe.

She finds Mabeuf's reticence charming. But what does he want? Does he want more than a conversation he might have with any one of his male friends?

Sabine understands that Mabeuf is a man who has to be coaxed, and before long she pushes him forward.

"Tell me why I'm here."

Mabeuf squirms.

"I'm quite taken with you."

"In what way?"

"I think you know."

"But it's possible I don't."

Mabeuf shrugs.

"You're a woman of great beauty."

Sabine gazes at him.

"Is that what you want?"

He tells her his compliments are sincere.

"I believe in sincerity," he says.

"How interesting."

"You make this difficult for me."

"Is it true you have a mistress?"

He looks uncomfortable now, his fingers pulling at his chin.

"I'm afraid the affair has run its course."

"Tell me her name."

Colette Gautier."

"Is she beautiful?"

"Yes, quite."

"Then you shouldn't leave her."

Mabeuf says Colette is much too simple.

"An empty head. It gets boring, you know."

"How amusing."

"Amusing? Why do you find it amusing?"

"What do you like about women?"

He pulls at his chin again.

"The usual things, I suppose."

"The usual enjoyments?"

"Yes of course."

"No, I think you're not truthful. I think you find the usual enjoyments unbearably dull."

His eyes are blank.

"Perhaps."

"What do you want from a woman?"

"I don't know. One is never certain."

"I know what you want. Is it possible I know?"

He blushes.

"Yes, why not?"

"I'll show you, if you like."

Mabeuf looks puzzled.

"What do you mean?"

"Would you like me to show you that I know what you want?"

"Yes."

"Touch yourself."

"What?"

"Your affair. What name should we use? Your asparagus. What did your mother call it?"

His voice is a whisper.

"My God."

"Tell me."

"My pipi."

"Yes, of course. Touch your pipi."

For a moment he does nothing. They sit there

with their eyes locked. And then Mabeuf slowly moves his hand to his lap.

He trembles as he does it. He looks right and left, his eyes wide in his excitement.

"Excited?"

"Yes."

"You have an erection, don't you?"

"Yes."

Sabine laughs.

"How lovely."

"My God."

"I must go now."

"Please . . ."

"No, darling, I must go."

"I must see you again."

"Yes, if you like."

"Where?"

"You might visit me."

*

From the beginning Mabeuf considers it a miracle. He visits her two days later at three o'clock in the afternoon.

Her flat in Rue de Rennes is comfortable but not luxurious. She sends the maid away and she pours cognac for Leon in the warm sitting room.

He's brought roses, a dozen red flowers to be arranged in a vase near one of the open windows.

"I like to walk in the Luxembourg," Sabine says.

She toys with the flowers. Is he looking at her? She wears a blue silk dress that's a bit tight around the hips. She feels his eyes on her body. Well, let him imagine things.

They talk. Leon's excitement is evident. His eyes are always upon her, his breathing rapid, his hands constantly twitching. He makes an attempt to sit quietly, to keep his equilibrium, but the air of sensuality in the room is too much for him.

Sabine is amused. She thinks how easy it is. She thinks of the mines in South America. Does he really own mines in South America? She likes his manner, his expensive tailoring, even the cut of his hair. An improvement, she thinks. Mabeuf is certainly an improvement.

The room is warm. Leon's forehead glistens with perspiration. Sabine wags a Japanese fan back and forth in front of her face.

"I must change," she says. "I must change my clothes. Why don't you come with me?"

Come with her? Come with her where? Leon shows his puzzlement.

"In the bedroom," she says. "I don't like to be alone."

She allows him to watch her disrobe. His eyes are wide, his cheeks flushed, his hands trembling as her body is revealed.

Sabine teases him, first with her breasts and then with her bottom. The blushing globes of her bottom. Leon stares. Does he murmur with excitement? Sabine glances at the mirror to consider the rouge on her lips.

"Does it bother you that I'm naked? I don't think people ought to hide their bodies."

He finds it difficult to talk.

"You're a goddess."

"Am I prettier than your mistress? I don't remember her name."

"Colette."

"Yes, Colette. Does she have pretty breasts?"

"Not as pretty as yours."

"You're a naughty boy. I can see your pipi is not behaving himself."

Leon groans.

"Forgive me."

"What do you want?" Sabine says.

His forehead glistens.

"I don't know."

"Would you like to make minette? Would you like to suck me? Yes, I think you'd like that."

She sits on the bench before her dressing table and she beckons to him. He goes to his knees, a sound of pleasure coming from his throat as he crawls towards her.

Sabine opens her thighs, her hands framing her dark nest, her eyes on Leon's face. She reveals it to him, her fingers pulling at the lips, opening her sex, showing him her clitoris, the red mouth below it.

"Is this what you want?"

His answer is a groan. As though in a drunken stupor, he lurches forward to use his mouth.

He's hungry for it. His face presses against her sex, his lips and tongue working at her flesh. She gazes down and watches it, her eyes on his head, his lips, his nose pressing against her thicket.

Not bad, she thinks.

Yes, it's good. She adores it. She always adores it when she has a tongue down there. A mount at her source. Oh yes.

She keeps him at it until she tires of it, and then she pushes him away and she closes her legs.

"Let me see it. Let me see your pipi."

Leon struggles with his flies, a madness in his face as he works to get himself exposed to Sabine.

His organ stands out quivering, an engaging curve, the cowl pulled back to show a dark red helmet.

She touches him with her foot, her toes stroking the shaft of his penis, Leon groaning as he watches it with mesmerized eyes.

Sabine is amused at how easy he is. She rubs her foot back and forth across his turgid organ. She can feel his flesh throbbing beneath her toes.

Leon groans. He spurts. He falls back as his penis continues spurting. She keeps her foot moving, her eyes hot as she watches the twitching and spurting, the pale white of it on his trousers.

Well, it's not bad, she thinks. Monsieur Leon Mabeuf is in good form. She likes a man with some life in his balls.

*

Sabine and Claude Orac are at a café table in St. Germain. On the sidewalk a clown is waving his arms and making horrible faces at the people who pass him.

Sabine wears a pink hat and she sips a Pernod.

Claude looks unhappy, uneasy to be seen with her.

"You're thoughtful," Sabine says.

He pulls out his gold watch.

"I can't stay long."

"Are you too busy for poor Sabine?"

"You know it's not that."

"You're afraid Amelie will catch you with me."

"Yes."

Sabine smiles. She thinks of them together, Amelie and Claude, Amelie on her back in her fluffy bed with her toes pointed at the ceiling.

"You're a charming man."

"Sabine, what's the purpose of this?"

"I thought we ought to know each other a little better. Don't you like me?"

"You're an astounding woman."

Sabine thinks of her friends. Is Amelie her friend or merely a convenience?

"Tell me about Leon Mabeuf."

Claude sighs.

"So that's it."

The clown on the sidewalk is waving his arms again.

"Tell me," Sabine says. "Are you intimate friends?"

"Certainly not. He's just a man I know."

"At the bourse?"

"Yes, at the bourse."

"And does Leon do well at the bourse?"

Claude tells her everything. Leon does well enough at the bourse. The mines in Chile are successful. Leon is a rich man.

"You mustn't tell him," Sabine says.

"About what?"

"About this meeting."

Claude is nervous again.

"Of course not."

"I like you. You might help me buy clothes some time. Would you like that? We needn't tell Amelie, of course. A few hours some afternoon.

Would it interest you?"

She teases him. She touches his hand. He looks at her fingers and then he closes his hand over hers.

"You're an astounding woman."

"When you have a free afternoon," Sabine says.

*

"Well, you have him," Amelie says.

"I do?"

"Leon has given the boot to Colette Gautier. Aren't you happy?"

"I don't know."

Amelie laughs.

"Sabine, darling, think of the mines."

The mines, the mines. Sabine thinks of the mines in South America. Leon sends a note and she agrees to go to the opera with him.

*

"What do you want from me?" Sabine says.

They sit in Sabine's flat a few minutes before midnight. She sips her cognac and then she leans back in her chair and she looks at Leon.

He shrugs.

"I'm not certain."

"Men are always so uncertain of things."

"Perhaps."

Leon's eyes never leave her. They remain silent for a long moment. There is no sound in the room except the ticking of the ormolu clock on the mantel. Only one lamp is lit, a lamp with a pink silk shade that casts a pink glow over everything.

Sabine crosses her legs, the left leg over the right, her left ankle turning.

"Tell me about Colette. What did you do with her?"

"Do with her?"

"How did you make love?"

A flush comes to Leon's face.

"It was quite ordinary."

"I don't believe it. I want you to tell me everything."

His voice is cracked.

"It's not possible."

"Well, we'll see."

They sit quietly again, neither of them moving, Sabine in the chair and Leon on the small sofa. Sabine looks at the room. She's in one of those times when she despises her furniture. Next week it will change again. This week she hates everything in the room. The porcelain figurines on the mantel seem particularly ugly to her. Indeed as ugly as her life. She thinks her life is ugly. Her comforts mean nothing. But how can she possible exist without them?

She looks at Leon and she sees that he's sweating, the perspiration evident on his forehead.

"Come to me. Sit at my feet."

He does it immediately, leaves the sofa to sit on the rug near her chair. She touches his face and in a moment he leans his head against her knees.

"Did you do this with Colette?"

"No."

Silence again. Not a sound in the room except the ticking of the clock.

Now Leon touches her leg, her left leg, the leg that crosses over the right leg, his finger touching her calf, his fingers running over the silk of her stocking, up and down her calf and down her ankle to touch the contours of her shoe.

She digs her pointed heel into his palm.

Then she pulls her foot away.

She uncrosses her legs. Her fingers tug at the hem of her dress and she slowly uncovers her thighs.

"I'm not wearing any drawers. See? Nothing at all. Go on, then. Yes, like that . . . sniff it first . . . I like to be sniffed, darling."

Her sex is wet. She teases him by making him stop, and then a moment later she pulls at his head again to make him continue.

His mouth is drenched with her syrup.

He buries his face in her sex.

Only silence now, only the ticking of the clock on the mantel.

*

The next afternoon Sabine assures Leon he will never be allowed to completely possess her.

His eyes are round.

"Dear God, why not?"

"Because I won't allow it."

He sits at her feet again, his hands running over her ankles, her calves, his fingers stroking her legs. He stares up at her with those round eyes.

He has no understanding of anything. He begs her. He kneels at her feet and he begs her like a young boy.

"Please, Sabine . . ."

"It's my wish."

"I can't bear it if you hate me."

"Darling, I don't hate you, I'm quite fond of you."

He groans as he kisses her legs.

Sabine quivers.

"Yes, I like that."

She strokes his face. She listens to the traffic on the boulevard. A horn sounds as Leon pushes his face between her thighs.

Yes, he accepts it now. Sabine opens her legs to his hungry mouth.

*

He sends flowers every day.

In a week he brings an emerald necklace to the flat in Rue de Rennes.

"It's lovely," Sabine says. "I'm sure it costs a fortune, but it's very extravagant and you ought to return it."

"No, I want you to have it. I also want you to travel with me."

"Travel to where?"

"To South America."

"You must be mad."

"I need you, Sabine. I must go to Chile to look after the family property and I want you with me."

She thinks of the mines. She holds the emerald necklace in her fingers and she thinks of the mines.

"For how long, Leon?"

"One year, perhaps two."

"It's impossible."

"I beg you."

In a month they leave Cherbourg by steamship. Sabine and Leon stand at the rail to wave goodbye to the people on the dock. Sabine wears the emerald necklace. She wears a new hat and the green of the hat is precisely the same as the green of the necklace.

Chapter Three

*

And now a child is running on the deck of the Reina del Pacifico.

Sabine sits in a white chair with the book she was reading closed in her lap. She wears a white gaucho hat, the hat she bought in Buenos Aires during the time she and Leon were there so many months ago.

The deck is crowded with passengers, people strolling by Sabine's chair, another child joining the first and the two of them running together from rail to rail.

Sabine thinks of her surprise about Leon. Why is she so surprised? The man is past sixty. People are mortal. Leon's heart is not good. But of course he might have told her in Paris; it was nasty of him not to tell her, or at least thoughtless.

At any rate it's not the sort of surprise she enjoys.

One of the two children is carried away somewhere and now only the first child remains: a small boy wearing a blue and white sailor suit and a hat with two ribbons that flap in the breeze. The boy in the sailor suit reminds Sabine of an old photograph of the family of the Czar of Russia. What was his name? She can't think of it; she can't remember. Did she see the photograph in a magazine or did one of her friends in Paris tell her about it? No, it was Uncle Hector. It was Uncle Hector in Paris who once showed the photograph to her. The Czar and his family. Sabine chides herself for being so ridiculous. There are no more Czars. Or maybe the Czars never existed. How does one know such things? Why does she think of the Czar's child? That little boy in the sailor suit, and this little boy in the sailor suit. The photograph of the Czar and his family and the little boy in the sailor suit sitting in front with his hands folded so peacefully in his lap. Sabine remembers they were all killed somewhere, murdered by the Bolsheviks. She remembers her Uncle Hector pointing his finger at the photograph and accusing someone. But accusing whom? The Czar or the Bolsheviks?

Sabine thinks: I hate politics. Yes I do.

But the child continues running back and forth on the deck with his ribbons flapping in the breeze. The boy is shouting now and his mother suddenly appears.

Sabine watches the young mother with her child, a young woman with blonde hair, bent over now as she tightens the strap that holds the boy's hat to his head.

A breeze again, a cool breeze that fans Sabine's face as she watches the boy and his mother.

Sabine considers the absence of marriage and children in her life.

A scent of jasmine comes from somewhere.

Sabine opens the book in her lap and then she closes it with a twitch of boredom.

The child is shouting again and once more Sabine looks at the young mother, at the young blonde woman bent over the boy with her derriére standing out to tantalize the male passengers.

She might be a widow, Sabine thinks. No, it's absurd, that blonde woman is certainly not a widow.

Once again Sabine feels the anxiety in her chest. Leon's illness. Her future. She must find a new benefactor.

The people on the deck are strolling again; for an interval the movement seemed to have stopped, but now the people are strolling again.

*

It's the money of course. Sabine knows very well what it is. She's an outsider here. Oh yes, they look at her with such interest in their eyes, but she's quite the outsider. She has the beauty, of course, but she's not at all vain about it. She wants their admiration; she wants the admiration of these fat geese, these matrons who stick their noses in the air at the idea that some woman on the ship is disturbing the equanimity of their husbands. Well, they have their purposes and Sabine has hers. Sabine believes a life ought to have some purpose. She tells herself she has a degree of humility about her life. Yes, they look at her. Her breasts are round and beautiful. Her figure is enough to bring a man to his knees. Her skin, the curves of her hips compensate for some of the ugliness in this ugly little world. Perhaps she's a clown. Am I a clown? Sabine does not want the mockery of the world. She does not think of herself as slow and stupid. She cries too much. She remembers all the weeping. She thinks of herself as one of those miserable sinners doomed to a life of tears. Does she want pity? She condemns the idea.

*

The ship's doctor, this young English doctor who calls himself Arthur Gordon, is on his knees on the floor of his cabin with his face buried between Sabine's widespread thighs.

Once again Sabine notices the doctor's hair is the color of sand.

She sits upright in a wooden chair with her arms on the arms of the chair and her thighs spread wide apart. Her skirt has been pulled up past her hips and below the waist she wears nothing but her shoes and stockings, the brown silk stockings rolled at their tops to cover her garters. These are the only stockings remaining from those she brought with her from Paris. All the others have been replaced by silk stockings bought in Buenos Aires and Santiago and Valparaiso, not as fine as Parisian stockings but perhaps a bit more durable.

Sabine closes her thighs against the head of the ship's doctor. Her stockings are gartered above her knees, but not high enough to keep the bare flesh of her thighs from rubbing against the doctor's ears.

She presses her thighs against his head and then she opens her thighs again to release him.

She looks around her at his cabin. The doctor's living quarters are immaculate, no sign of disorder, nothing out of place, the cover of the small bed drawn tight, the small desk uncluttered and with no more than three books stacked neatly in a corner.

He's an innocent, Sabine thinks.

She pats the doctor's head.

"You're a hungry little boy."

The doctor pulls his mouth away from her sex no more than an inch, no more than enough to free his lips to speak.

"What?"

Sabine can feel his warm breath on her clitoris.

"Never mind, darling. Just keep doing it, will you?"

His tongue returns. Much too hesitant and not at all interesting. But he's persistent enough, like a young Celt chopping away at a stubborn oak tree, his tongue chopping at her clitoris until Sabine is forced to close her eyes and grip his head and hide the shuddering of her knees.

When the doctor finally pulls his face away, Sabine keeps her thighs apart. A flush comes to the doctor's face as he gazes at her sex.

Sabine touches the dark curls on her mount with her fingertips.

"You shouldn't look so surprised."

He lifts his eyes to her face.

"What do you mean?"

"You've seen a woman's parts before, haven't you? Now let me see yours. Stand up and let me see it. You don't want to keep hiding it, do you?"

The flush in his face takes on a deeper color. The doctor rises. His braces come down. His trousers. His drawers. His penis rises like a pink scimitar, curved and rising upward, the straining arc of an organ at the edge of explosion.

"Why aren't you married?" Sabine says. "Don't you like English girls?"

She touches him. She touches the base of his penis. She fondles his fat testicles.

"What?"

"Aren't you listening? I asked if you like English girls."

He trembles.

"Yes of course."

"Well, you ought to. Are you rich? Is your family in England rich?"

"Lord no."

"Pity."

"What?"

"Never mind."

"Let me make love to you."

Sabine laughs.

"You want to put this inside me?"

"Yes."

"That's not possible."

"Of course it is."

"No, it's not. I won't have it. Don't you see, darling? It wouldn't be any good."

His face is so pink. An Englishman pink in his face and pink in the balls. Such fat healthy testicles he has. Sabine holds his fat testicles in her left hand and she begins stroking his penis with her right hand.

The doctor groans.

In a moment he's gushing, blushing and gushing, blushing and spurting. Sabine holds his affair pointed to one side to avoid ruining her dress.

The doctor groans again as she squeezes his

essentials.

It's not possible, Sabine thinks. He's not rich and it's not at all possible.

*

So there it is. Sabine is constantly torn between her desire for freedom and her need for a life of luxury. She spends hours thinking about her destiny, about the destiny of her friends, about the destiny of people she hardly knows, about the destiny of anyone that chooses to cross the stage in front of her eyes.

She hates the past. She does not want to look inside herself. Of course it's not always possible; there are times when a woman needs to see more in her mirror than the shape of her mouth.

Sabine, where is the great love?

Certainly there is no great love in the back of Leon's eyes. Or in the back of the eyes of the young English doctor. Sabine shudders as she feels the first hint of a creeping destruction.

But never mind. She smiles now as she thinks of her own wickedness. She adores the taste of red wine on her lips. She remembers a rendezvous on a train in the south of France. She remembers the motion of the train. Who was it? Not Daurez. Was it Georges Baader? Well, what difference does it make now? One has the pleasure of the memory and certainly that's more than the pleasure of the moment.

*

If the English doctor is not suitable, then what course does Sabine pursue?

On the foredeck one afternoon a slim gentleman with black eyebrows introduces himself as Señor Fernando Jimenez.

"At your service, madame."

In the most perfect French.

Sabine is surprised.

"But you're not French."

Señor Jimenez reveals himself as a Chilean diplomat, a member of the Foreign Office, a member of an old family, a member of the Santiago Riding Club, an afficianado of the novels of Montherlant, an aide of sorts to his ambassador in Paris.

"How interesting," Sabine says.

The eyes of Jimenez are interesting, his dark and staring and reverent eyes.

"Madame is most beautiful."

His eyes are on Sabine's breasts. He talks of Paris, his hands waving in the air, his head nodding, his eyes returning again and again to Sabine's uncovered throat.

They make a turn around the deck of the ship, Jimenez constantly talking, the seabirds in the sky constantly gliding.

"And your husband, madame? Is he enjoying the voyage?"

"I have no husband."

"How wonderful."

"Wonderful, señor?"

"Merely an expression."

"Is your wife travelling to Paris?"

"In a few months, perhaps."

Sabine is amused.

"I must go to my cabin now."

He begs to see her again. His eyes reek with his reverence and there is no way she can resist it. She agrees to a meeting.

"In a few days, perhaps."

He kisses her hand, his neck bent, his lips turned out, his tongue tickling her fingers.

When Sabine returns to the cabin, Leon is furious.

"I witnessed everything."

"Leon, don't be stupid."

"Sabine, I witnessed everything."

"There was nothing to witness."

His eyes are red.

"Who is he?"

"I don't know. Just another passenger."

"I won't have it."

Sabine says nothing.

What an old fool, she thinks. What a silly old fool.

Later they sit on the deck and Leon begins talking about the Germans on the ship.

"All Nazis," Leon says.

The sea birds are flying again. Are they near the coast of Peru? A small boy with a horn stands at the rail with his eyes on the water.

"All spies," Leon says.

Sabine is amused.

"I don't care. Do you really care, Leon?"

Sabine is not interested in politics. She's always bored by political talk. She finds the Germans so amusing. All that ranting produced by beer and cabbage.

When Sabine rises, she has the breeze in her hair.

"I think I'll take a walk."

"I'll go with you," Leon says.

"No, I'd rather be alone."

His eyes are begging. She refuses him. She turns and walks.

Sabine walks off the deck to find the doctor's cabin. Men turn and look at her as she steps off the deck and into the long corridor that runs past the lounge. She wears white cotton and the cotton molds her thighs.

When she knocks on Doctor Gordon's door, he opens it immediately.

"You're late."

"Darling, I don't care."

"Then you're cruel."

But he's happy to see her. She laughs at him. She sits down in one of the feeble chairs in his cabin and she crosses her legs. He stands there with his sad-looking eyes on her legs and she sees that it's already begun.

"You don't look well," she says.

"I think you're driving me mad."

"Now don't be silly again. I don't like it when you're silly. You don't want me to be angry, do you?"

"No, I don't want that."

I don't have much time. You shouldn't be standing, I think. You don't want to stand, do you?"

He groans.

"I don't know."

"Kneel, darling."

His face is so pink. He lowers himself slowly, his shoulders dropping, his body dropping until

· 40 ·

his knees touch the floor.

Sabine looks at the floor and she sees that after all the floor is clean, certainly much cleaner than the floor in the cabin she shares with Leon.

She makes Doctor Gordon crawl to her. There's no need to say anything because it's been done before and he knows the doing of it. He's sweating now, the sweat showing on his high pink forehead as he crawls over the floor with his eyes on Sabine's legs.

Finally he arrives. He kisses her legs. Sabine sits motionless as Doctor Gordon runs his lips over the silk of her stockings.

"I want your help," she says.

"My help?"

"There's a passenger named Fernando Jimenez. He's a diplomat, I think. I want you to find out everything you can about him and then tell me what you learn. Will you do that, darling?"

"Fernando Jimenez."

"Yes, that's it."

"All right."

"You're sweet."

She opens her thighs to his face. Does he murmur something? Sabine shudders as his tongue begins tickling the insides of her thighs.

Chapter Four

*

Leon has arranged their dinner at the captain's table.

There are twelve people and Sabine is pleased to have the captain at her right elbow.

The captain is happy with his table, his eyes moving from one elegant woman to the next, his moustache redder than ever in the yellow light, his lips moist as he banters with Sabine in French while his eyes stare boldly at her breasts.

Across the table, Leon is sweating as he watches Sabine and the captain.

Sabine considers the captain as a potential benefactor. She considers his English mouth, his red moustache. She might live in Paris while he tours the oceans. But of course the Reina del Pacifico is not the grandest ship at sea. Not grand at all. And maybe when the captain goes ashore in Southampton his only interest is a month on his farm in Cornwall. What would I do in Cornwall? Sabine thinks. I'll walk in the village and talk to the dogs. And his red moustache is ferocious; oh yes, the red moustache is ferocious.

Sabine decides the idea is absurd.

A basket of knitting and a tin of tobacco, Sabine thinks. It's really absurd.

Sabine, darling, you're an odd one, aren't you? You're a stranger to yourself.

She feels uncertain about everything now. The

people in the dining room seem so dull and unreal. Sabine struggles to keep awake as she sits there staring at them. She feels a numbness of the flesh, a slow dying that goes on and on.

It's all turning to mud, she thinks. One minute she enjoys herself and the next minute she has the awful feeling the world is disintegrating. She suddenly finds it difficult to breathe. The suffocating sensation lasts only a moment and then she quickly recovers.

She looks at Leon again. She does not want to be an old woman counting her degradations. We all have our secrets. All these people have their dark memories that still confuse them.

You must be relentless, Sabine thinks.

Then she feels a knot of hostility towards Leon. I'm not gone yet, Sabine thinks. She has her spirit and she's not gone yet.

*

This is a grey day.

Leon has a cold and he sits with a peaked cap on his head and misery in his eyes.

Sabine taunts him about his jealousy.

"You behave like a child."

The sea birds are more numerous now. The ship is off the coast of Peru and the sea birds have become raucous and frenzied in the grey sky.

A man and a woman pass the chairs where Sabine and Leon are sitting. The Italian couple. Sabine recognizes the woman.

"I feel horrible," Leon says.

Sabine arranges the sweater she wears on her

shoulders.

"I think you enjoy your jealousy."

"It's not true."

"Yes, it is true. Do you remember that time in Santiago? That young porter?"

Sabine is amused as she remembers Leon hiding in that closet while she had the young hotel porter on the bed in that scruffy little room that smelled of fried onions.

"Do you want a girl, Leon?"

"I feel too horrible."

"I'll get one for you in Lima. There ought to be girls available in Lima."

Sabine looks forward to an excursion in Lima. The ship will dock in Callao for three days and she'll have solid ground under her feet again.

"I'll find a little doll for you," Sabine says. "One of those Peruvian girls with a shapely behind."

*

Of course Leon is a child and Sabine is completely aware of it. There are times when she feels so motherly towards him. He seems so ravaged and destroyed these days, so utterly miserable now that he's lost the family fortune.

But the boasting continues, the dull evenings with Sabine embellishing her beauty and Leon gazing at her as he boasts of his accomplishments. Does he care about her suffering? Sabine has learned to ignore his senseless complaints, his whining at moments when silence would be more pleasing.

He adores the way she treats him; he adores his

degradation. Sabine is amused at the way his eyes roll when he has his pleasure. What a disgrace he is. How ridiculous that he finds himself so precious. She hates this vile ship. How awful that a black fate has brought her to a stuffy cabin at the end of the world.

"Darling, what is it you want?" Sabine shudders as she suddenly remembers a photograph of an old hag in a dirty street.

I don't want anything. I want everything.

*

In the evening a dance in the ship's ballroom, the passengers crowding under the crystal chandeliers. Sabine finds it pleasant. She likes crowds if the people are elegant. The orchestra plays a fast waltz and Leon shakes his head and says the dance will kill him.

"Find someone else."

Sabine dances with the English doctor.

She wants a life of color and enhancement.

Some of the men are handsome and she's aware of the way they look at her.

Then the orchestra plays a tango and suddenly the captain is there to take her arm.

He smiles at her beneath his red moustache.

"Enchanting, madame."

How awful he is. But Sabine is pleased at the way he dances, at his white uniform, at the gold braid on his epaulets and the gold buttons and the jealous eyes of the other women. And he's a skillful dancer. Sabine enjoys the moment, the whirling dance, the whirling of the chandeliers.

"You're a lovely woman," the captain says.

His eyes are on her breasts.

"Do you really think so?"

"You're the most beautiful woman on my ship."

Sabine laughs. After the dance is finished she returns to Leon.

"He's charming."

"He's a buffoon," Leon says.

Sabine is amused by the male ego. Leon is such a lamb. And what are you, Sabine? A simple shepherdess? She tells herself she needs to make certain decisions about her life. It's no longer enough to enjoy the way they feed upon her. She needs to exercise self-denial; she needs the good sense of maturity. Their promises are worth nothing to her any more. Sabine shudders as she thinks of all the broken promises. She looks around her at all these people, these passengers gorged with rich food. What eagerness they have. They arouse themselves. Each day is a divine worship to a great emptiness. Come to the Mass, they say. Oh, she's quite aware of it. She's not that silly that she doesn't have a certain vigilance about things.

You're as much an animal as the rest of them, she thinks. You're an alley cat.

Yes, an alley cat. A bewildered animal in the shadows of a decrepit church.

*

Now it is three days before the ship docks at Callao and in the afternoon on the deck Sabine receives a note from the captain.

Dear Miss Boulanger.

An invitation to visit the captain in his cabin.

The young sailor who brought the note stands with his eyes on the sea. Does he know the contents of the note? Sabine gazes at the front of the sailor's white trousers.

She returns the note unanswered.

She does not want the captain.

The Italians are on deck again, the Italian couple, the woman like a stick walking with her arm linked in the arm of her husband.

An hour later, as Sabine stands near the stern of the ship, she sees a grimy young sailor cleaning one of the winches. The sailor's clothes are soiled and he has grease on his arms.

Sabine suddenly decides she wants him. She beckons to the sailor and in a moment he approaches her.

"Can I help you, madam?"

When Sabine explains the sort of help she requires, the sailor's eyes become round.

Sabine offers him money. She names a price.

Now his eyes are on her breasts.

He agrees.

"I'll follow you," Sabine says. "We need to find a place, don't we?"

He leads her to a door, and then to a stairway, and then down below the deck to an alcove near the engine room.

The noise of the engines is like the heavy thudding of the heart of a monster.

The sailor smiles; Sabine can smell the stink of sweat and engine oil on his muscular body.

She gives him the money. He seems mesmerized as he takes the folded notes and slips them into one of his grimy pockets.

Now Sabine wants what she's paid for: one pays and one receives. She undoes his buttons and in a moment she has his organ and his testicles out in the air.

The engines of the ship continue throbbing.

Sabine handles the sailor, examines his essentials. He seems healthy enough. His penis is erect now, like a thick truncheon in her hand.

Sabine turns. She lifts her dress and she pulls her drawers down and then she bends over a large pipe to offer herself to the sailor.

Are the engines louder now? Sabine shudders as she feels the hands of the sailor on her buttocks.

His fingers.

He drives his organ inside her sex, pushing inside as Sabine groans, but of course the groan is drowned by the noise of the engines and the groan means nothing.

The sailor begins thrusting.

He's lusty enough.

Sabine's eyes are closed.

The ship's engines are pounding in Sabine's ears.

Pounding as the sailor is pounding.

Sabine has an orgasm as the sailor spends inside her.

Her eyes are closed. She hangs over the pipe with her eyes closed and now the beating of Sabine's heart is as loud as the beating of the engines.

*

Sabine is crying again.

She lies alone on the bed in the cabin and she weeps. She tells herself that she's an animal. Now she sees herself as a depraved female wolf, a beast with bloodshot eyes and fangs. And then the next moment she feels powerless again, powerless and perspiring. What a dread she has of these long days. She hates the silence in the cabin. Not a human voice to be heard, nothing but the creaking of the ship and the occasional call of a sea bird. There must be someone. Sabine, you have a weak head. She hates Leon. She has a great hatred for him now. What he really wants is a wife, someone to share these sweaty sheets without any complaints.

Oh yes, the seagulls are crying again.

Sabine is too lazy to turn her head to the porthole. She imagines the birds hovering over the ship, perching on the railings.

Are they Peruvian birds?

Then she hears voices again, the voices of two ladies giggling at something as they pass in the corridor.

A shudder passes through Sabine. She turns her head to the pillow and once again she begins crying.

*

Another day. The salon is crowded now. A sudden bad turn in the weather has pushed these people into the large room. Outside the windows the sea is grey and the sky is grey and enormous clouds have settled over the world without permission.

Sabine finds a chair in the salon. She hears the wood creaking and for a moment she's frightened. She tries to get comfortable, squirms in her chair, arranges her legs.

The salt air is in the salon. Sabine is tired of it. Such a long way to Cherbourg and she's already tired of it. She brings a book out of her purse, an old novel by Bourget purchased in a bookstore in Santiago, the leaves still uncut and the book still unread. The salon is too noisy, too stuffy. But she's bored with the sea. She cuts the pages with a small knife. She tries to concentrate on the novel, the words . . .

A shudder now as she thinks of Leon dying.

How will it happen? Will she be there at the end?

The woman in the novel seems so trivial: a lady from Lyon with fluttering hands. Ah well, it could be me, Sabine thinks.

What does she want from life? What does anyone want from life except a lack of misery? Is she to be blamed for anything? A woman leads her life according to her circumstances. Then why does she feel so guilty? How silly it is. It's not her fault that Leon is dying. Has she provided him any joy?

And she can't be blamed for amusing herself with that sailor.

Dear God, those animal thrusts, the engines and those animal thrusts.

Now she finds her fingers twitching. She hates rings and her fingers are bare.

Suddenly her breath is short; a sudden anxiety stuffs her chest.

The people in the salon seem so dull. Small people with such small lives.

Then Sabine has an illusion the ship has stopped moving. Everything is suddenly fixed, everything in the universe is suddenly frozen in place.

Is she trapped here, trapped off the coast of Peru in the midst of nothing?

She has a moment of dizziness. Then a smell of engine oil comes into the salon and she can't help thinking of the engines again. She recovers and she looks around her. Has anyone noticed? The chattering in the salon goes on as usual. A group of men at the bar are absorbed in their cognacs. Or whiskies. Are they Americans? One of them is looking at her.

Sabine looks away. She looks at the windows, at the clouds.

She reads; or she tries to read. The words don't make any sense.

No, she wants to stretch her legs. She stands and walks. Now the men at the bar are definitely looking at her. She continues walking, but only to the door of the salon.

She gazes at the sea through the glass.

What she needs is amusement. A sea voyage is so boring. Even the birds are boring. In the beginning she liked them; she thought them amusing. But now it's always the same: the birds gliding and turning and gliding again.

She hates the passengers. Don't they know Leon is dying?

Someone at the bar laughs.

Sabine stands with her annoyance, her

indecision, uncertain whether to go outside or sit down again.

The afternoon is always the worst time.

Suddenly outside on the deck Señor Jimenez appears. He walks like a marionette. He sees Sabine at the door of the salon and he immediately comes forward with a limp smile.

Once again Sabine sees the reverence in his eyes.

His black cravat does look distinguished.

"My dear Madame Boulanger. Is there any little service you require? Can I help you, madame?"

Sabine remembers the sailor who asked that, the same words, the same offer of assistance.

Señor Jimenez talks. He says he's been searching for Sabine on deck. He has a slight blush in his cheeks and now Sabine notices that his cravat is askew, turned a bit too much to the left.

She laughs. She taunts him.

"You're silly," Sabine says.

The blush deepens.

"Silly, madame?"

"What do you want?"

But she enjoys his reverence, the look of respectful ecstasy in his eyes. She admires the way his head is inclined, like a bird of sorts, an exotic tropical bird.

Sabine moves back to the interior of the salon and she sits down again.

Are they looking at her?

Jimenez approaches her like a lost dog. His hands are twitching. Sabine nods at the seat beside her and he sits down with a look of gratitude in his face.

Sabine shifts in her chair. At least it's an amusement. It's a dreary day after all and one needs the amusement.

She glances at the bar.

"What do you do to keep busy?" she says.

Jimenez stares at her.

"I read."

"Read what?"

"Old newspapers. I enjoy reading old newspapers."

How quaint he is.

Sabine laughs at him. He looks at her and in a moment he begins laughing too.

His teeth are so white.

*

Sabine lies on her bed in her cabin. Leon is out somewhere and Sabine is thankful for the silence. She feels as though she's floating in a dream. The cabin is stuffy, an airless room that creaks at intervals as the ship rolls in the sea. She wants to open the porthole but she's too weak.

Oh Sabine.

She thinks of Leon and she wonders where he might be. She feels so listless. It's another dull day and nothing seems worthwhile.

The sheet is damp enough to be an annoyance.

Is there anyone who is happy every day? Truly happy?

Now a creaking sound again, the bed creaking as the room moves.

Leon is much too emotional. His heart has been worn down, worn to the point of exhaustion by his endless turmoil.

Sabine looks at the porthole, at the empty sky, the blue always so constant.

She thinks of love. Does she love Leon? She thinks of the moments of tenderness with Leon. Of course he's been a necessity. Sabine, you're a lazy bitch and now Leon is dying.

The bed makes a creaking sound again.

*

Señor Fernando Jimenez stands naked in his cabin.

"How did you know?"

"Your eyes."

"My eyes?"

"You have the eyes of a servant."

Jimenez blushes.

His eyes are fixed on Sabine. She stands as naked as Jimenez, her breasts like a pair of ripe mangoes, her legs standing apart to emphasize the prominence of her dark thicket, the dark patch of fur at the apex of her white thighs.

Now there is music from somewhere, an aria from La Traviata.

"How amusing," Sabine says.

"Amusing?"

"The music."

"It's the idiot in the next cabin. His phonograph."

"But I like it."

"We'll be in Callao in a few hours."

"Thank God."

"Let me kiss you."

"As you wish."

He comes forward, but rather than kiss her mouth he falls to his knees and he begins kissing her ankles. First the left ankle and then the right ankle. Sabine finally pushes him away with her foot.

"Bring me some brandy."

Jimenez hurries to a corner of the cabin.

Sabine cups her left breast in her left hand, her thumb and forefinger pulling at her nipple as she looks at the spare cabin.

But it's only a cabin, she thinks. He might have a castle in Chile. In the Andes? Are there castles in the Andes? Or a large house in Santiago. I don't want to live in Santiago. He has a wife in Santiago. No, the wife will travel to Paris. But the cabin is so unimpressive. So empty. The house in Santiago might be nothing more than a cottage.

When Jimenez returns with the brandy, his organ is erect and vibrating. His lips are wet as he gazes at Sabine's breasts. He hands her the glass of brandy. In his other hand he holds something.

"What's that?" Sabine says.

"A leash."

Sabine nods. And a collar. She can see the collar in his hand.

"Yes, that's clever."

Jimenez kneels at her feet.

The ship rolls as Sabine leans over Jimenez to turn the leather collar and buckle it around his neck.

The leash is attached to the collar with a metal ring.

Sabine pulls at the leash.

"Come, we'll have a little walk."

She walks him about the cabin.

Jimenez grunts as he crawls over the floor of the cabin on his hands and knees. At intervals Sabine pulls at the leash, pulls at it hard to keep his head up.

Finally she stops the walking and she stands over him.

"You're a pretty dog, aren't you? My little bow-wow. Does my little bow-wow have a pretty tongue?"

Sabine moves her legs apart and in a moment Jimenez is there with his eyes bright and his nose and mouth pressed against her sex.

Sabine looks down at his nose. She moves her hips in a slow churning, her clitoris rubbing against his nose, her sex wetting his upturned face.

She pulls at the leash again.

"Keep the tongue moving. Don't you dare stop moving it."

It's not certain, Sabine thinks. The world of a diplomat is much too uncertain. She pushes her pelvis forward, her eyes on the head of Jimenez, on his leather collar, on his nose pressing into the dark forest that hides her sex.

Chapter Five

*

In the woman Sabine lives the ancient ghost of Sabine the child.

One summer day in the year 1916 the war comes to the town of Vouziers and Sabine's parents are killed by a German artillery shell.

Long live the tricolor.

Sabine is an orphan.

The priest throws holy water on the caskets.

The mayor of Vouziers arranges to have Sabine sent to Paris to live with her mother's sister.

The memory is the memory of a grey time, the noise of the wheels of the train as Sabine travels from Vouziers to Paris.

The train is crowded with wounded soldiers.

Sabine is to live with her Aunt Marthe and Uncle Hector. Sabine is unhappy at the prospect, but the aunt and the uncle are all she has. Completely alone, Sabine thinks. I'm completely alone.

A soldier with a white bandage around his head continues to show his yellow teeth as he smiles at her.

Sabine turns her attention to the window, to the passing countryside, to the sound of the wheels. She remembers the house in Paris, the house with high walls around it, the garden with large trees that obscure the neighborhood, the iron gate to keep out stray dogs and vagrants. A looming house. Sabine remembers it from the time she was there as a child. She remembers the inside of the house as dark and mysterious, the look of a cloister, the interior furnished with red velvet and red brocade and thick carpets covering the wooden floors.

And her aunt and uncle are bizarre. They never go out and they receive few visitors, odd visitors, pretty women wearing garish clothes, men with a look of guilt in their eyes.

Sabine remembers the murmuring and whispering and the rustling of silk in the drawing room.

How old was she? Ten? She lived in that house nearly an entire summer while her parents were in Normandy.

Does her aunt still scold the maids? When the weather was nice Aunt Marthe sat in the garden with Hector. Sabine remembers the stillness of the garden, the occasional chirp of a bird in one of the large trees.

Aunt Marthe liked Sabine to be naked in the house. Aunt Marthe undressed Sabine and bathed her. Sabine would play in Aunt Marthe's bedroom while Aunt Marthe changed her clothes. Sabine remembers Aunt Marthe's hands, the stroking of her skin.

I don't want it, Sabine thinks.

But she has no one else now. Sabine is sixteen and she has no one else.

Not even a cat. The poor cat was killed by the same artillery shell.

When Sabine looks at the bandaged soldier again, he's still smiling at her.

Finally the train arrives in Paris in a cloud of

steam and the orphan Sabine is welcomed by her aunt and uncle. They kiss her cheeks and she returns the kisses and now for the first time Sabine has a sudden feeling of delicious comfort.

"So many wounded soldiers," Marthe says. "Hector, I'm so thankful you're past the age for it."

"I'll be called before Christmas."

"I don't believe it. Sabine, darling, you must think of us as your parents."

In the taxi Sabine can smell her aunt's perfume, an exotic scent that reminds Sabine of certain forbidden novels that were lost with her mother and father and the poor little cat.

Sabine's Aunt Marthe is not at all like Sabine's mother.

During the first hours, both Marthe and Hector are solicitous, kindly toward Sabine, their eyes on Sabine, continually questioning Sabine about her comforts.

At dinner in the evening they urge her to eat, smile at her and she nibbles at her food.

The two maids are like shadows.

Marthe smiles at Sabine. Marthe talks to Hector in a low voice, talks about Sabine as Sabine watches and listens.

Then Marthe talks directly to Sabine again.

"You've become beautiful, darling."

Marthe's pearls are dazzling.

"You've developed," Marthe says. "You're no longer a small child. Isn't that true, Hector? Don't you see how beautiful Sabine has become?"

Hector nods.

"Yes, she's a beauty."

They drink red wine, the wine swirling in each glass, the red wine so lovely on the lips.

Sabine is tired and she wants to have a bath and go to bed.

"Please, Aunt Marthe . . ."

Hector's eyes are always on Sabine, his moustache wet now by the red wine he drinks.

"Not yet," Marthe says to Sabine. "You must have more wine with us. Hector and I are so happy to see you again."

The red wine swirls again, a thick red wine swirling in the warm room, swirling in Sabine's glass.

Sabine begs to have her bath.

Marthe is amused.

Finally Marthe leads Sabine to the bathroom to get the bath ready. The towels are brought. A maid carries a fresh bar of soap in a dish. Marthe sends the maid away and she fusses to get Sabine's bath ready for her.

"I never had a child," Marthe says. "I always wanted a daughter of my own."

At last Marthe leaves and the bathroom door is closed. Sabine undresses and she slides into the hot tub with a sigh of relief.

Sabine dozes in the heavy comfort of the hot bath.

Then she opens her eyes and she begins to wash her body with the soap. She has a strange sensation that she's being watched. But from where? She tells herself to stop being so silly. She stands in the tub and she slides the bar of soap over her breasts and over her belly and over her breasts again.

Suddenly the bathroom door opens and Marthe walks in with her silk dress rustling and her eyes on Sabine's dripping body.

Marthe's eyes move up and down as she smiles at Sabine.

"Do you remember how I used to bathe you?"

When Sabine leaves the tub, Marthe holds the large towel, dries Sabine, rubs her body everywhere.

Sabine shudders as her aunt rubs the towel over her naked body.

Marthe laughs.

"When you were here as a child you didn't have breasts like these. Not these lovely breasts."

Sabine's breasts are trembling, the tip shaking as Marthe rubs them with the towel.

"We had pleasure with you," Marthe says. "We watched you run naked about the house. Like a little elf."

Marthe's eyes are bright. She continues rubbing Sabine's breasts with the towel until Sabine's nipples are stiff.

Sabine's nipples are like berries, two red berries at the tips of her breasts, swollen now with all the rubbing and shaking and attention they receive.

"You're beautiful," Marthe says. "Such a lovely girl."

Marthe's eyes are so bright.

Now Marthe kisses Sabine's shoulder. She fondles Sabine's breasts; she toys with Sabine's nipples.

Sabine shudders as her breasts are stroked by Marthe's pink hands.

"I like to be naked," Marthe says. "Sometimes I like to be naked in the house."

Marthe's cheeks are flushed. Sabine trembles as Marthe continues kissing her neck and shoulders, continues fondling her breasts and stroking her nipples and laughing softly against her ear. Marthe seems intoxicated, her fingers fluttering over Sabine's body, her fingers always stroking as she murmurs her pleasure.

Now a hand on Sabine's hip, the hand moving up and down.

"What a pretty little nest."

They both look down at Sabine's belly, at the dark patch of fur at the joining of her thighs.

"I adore you," Marthe says.

Sabine feels as though she's in a dream. She's drowsy from the wine and the hot bath and now her aunt has brought a hot turmoil into her mind.

Finally Marthe pulls away from Sabine.

"You don't need more than a nightgown, darling. We'll be going to bed soon and you don't need more than that."

Sabine shudders again as her aunt helps her get the cotton nightgown over her shoulders.

They return to the living room. Hector is still drinking wine. His face is flushed red in the light of the fireplace. He looks at them and he laughs.

"Well, the bath went on forever, didn't it?"

Sabine quivers under his amusement. Marthe makes Sabine sit down near the fire to drink more wine. Once again Sabine is staring at the red wine as it swirls in her glass.

Marthe sits on the arm of the chair occupied by Hector. Marthe's ankles are slender, covered by dark silk that now catches the light of the fire. Sabine sits facing them and she can see her aunt's thighs outlined by the silk dress she wears.

It's a marriage, Sabine thinks. Marthe and Hector. Hector and Marthe. My aunt and my uncle.

"Sabine is so beautiful," Marthe says to Hector. "Such a beauty in her bath. Such lovely breasts."

Hector is amused, his eyes fixed on Sabine.

Sabine protests.

"Please, Aunt Marthe . . ."

But Marthe continues.

"Breasts like ripe apples, Hector. She has the tits of an angel. Do you remember how you used to play with her when she was a child?"

The walls are so red. Sabine shudders as she stares at the red walls.

Sabine feels the flush in her face. She feels the excitement now. She continues drinking with them. Hector's eyes never leave her. Marthe hums an old melody as Sabine stares at the wine in her glass.

At last Marthe agrees that it's time for bed.

"You'll have the divan in our bedroom," Marthe says. "We haven't had time to prepare a room for you."

Sabine is unsteady as she rises from her chair. She's had too much of the red wine. Are the maids still awake?

The bedroom is furnished in red, as red as the other rooms in the house, red walls and a red carpet and red drapes and red lampshades. The bed is immense and the divan against the wall near the bed is certainly large enough to be comfortable.

"Just this one night," Marthe says to Sabine. "Your own room will be ready tomorrow."

Sabine is troubled by her aunt's room, the strangeness of it, the red light, the scent of her aunt's perfume. On one of the walls hangs a large photograph of Marthe and Hector at the time of their wedding.

Sabine hurries to get under the sheet that covers the divan while Marthe begins to undress.

Hector sits in a chair and does nothing.

Sabine slowly yields to the urge to look at her aunt. She keeps her eyes covered with one of her arms, but she peers under the arm to look at Marthe as Marthe slowly undresses.

Marthe continually talks to Hector, her voice soft, her fingers working at her dress. She undresses without any haste, stopping at intervals to look at herself in the large mirror opposite the bed.

But soon the undressing is finished and Sabine sees her aunt completely naked. Marthe exhibits herself, the ripe flesh a dark pink in the red light of the lamps, her heavy breasts jiggling as she walks about the room.

Does Marthe know Sabine is looking at her? Marthe fondles her breasts in front of the mirror. Her dark nipples look enormous to Sabine.

Hector sits there watching everything. His eyes are on Marthe, on her flanks, on her full breasts.

Sabine quivers at the sight of her aunt's lush body, Marthe's ripeness. Sabine shudders beneath the sheet that covers her on the divan, so close to Marthe that when Marthe turns Sabine is awed by the deep split between the globes of Marthe's rear.

Like an animal, Sabine thinks. Her aunt is a female animal.

And why not?

Now Marthe deliberately walks near the divan. Sabine is overwhelmed by the nearness of her aunt's naked body, Marthe's heavy breasts, the slop of her belly, the forest of dark hair that covers her sex.

Still dressed, still seated in his chair, Hector continues to watch everything.

Sabine continues to peer at them with slitted eyes.

Now Marthe sits down in a chair near the large mirror. Sabine can see Marthe's body in the mirror, Marthe's fat nipples, the dark points extended, the swollen breasts quivering with her movements.

Marthe looks at Hector.

"Well, you want to undress, don't you? Are you going to sit there like that all night?"

The room is too warm, the warmth made heavy by the two red lamps that cast an eerie glow over everything.

Sabine watches Hector as he rises to undress. He's not that old. Her body shudders as she watches him. When his trousers are off, Sabine can see that his organ is erect in his drawers.

Then suddenly his penis appears through the slit in his drawers and Sabine's heart is pounding.

That fat red knob.

Her uncle's organ protrudes out of the opening in his drawers like a huge club. A weapon.

Sabine is frightened by his penis, frightened by the size of it, the menacing aspect of it.

She's never seen one before, not like this, not erect and throbbing and so frightening in its aggressive posture.

Now Hector scratches the base of his penis, and then he pulls at his testicles to get them hanging out of the slit in his drawers.

Marthe is amused at the state of her husband's organ.

"You're ready for it, aren't you? Those balls look full enough."

Marthe opens her legs to show Hector her sex, the hairy cave between her thighs.

Hector smiles.

"You'll get what you want," he says.

He strokes his organ with his hand, his fingers pushing and pulling, covering and uncovering the fat red knob at the end of it.

Marthe laughs at him.

"I won't complain. You won't find me complaining."

Sabine shudders as she watches them.

Hector moves to Marthe now, kneels at her feet as she opens her thighs. Marthe murmurs with approval as he leans forward to get his mouth on her sex.

Sabine holds her breath as she gazes at the pink tongue of her uncle, his pink tongue flapping against the dark sex of her aunt, his pink tongue licking in the hairy slit like a probing serpent.

"Yes, it's good," Marthe says.

His mouth works at her, his lips and tongue working at her sex.

Sabine can see his organ erect between his thighs, his hairy testicles dangling below his organ, his hairy thighs, the play of light on the muscles of his legs.

Marthe pats his head.

"On the bed, old man. It's better on the bed. I want that sausage inside me."

But Hector continues sucking her sex.

Sabine's heart beats in her chest as she stares at them, at their skin so pink in the red light.

It's madness, Sabine thinks.

She hears the sound of his sucking. She watches the face of her aunt, the mouth of her aunt as Marthe licks her lips.

Sabine shudders as she watches her aunt's face.

Now Marthe twists her body in the chair and she laughs as she manages to get her hand on Hector's organ, a soft laugh as she slowly strokes his affair with her fingers.

"Enough," Marthe says. "I'll kick you if you don't stop it."

They rise up and kiss each other. Belly against belly, their lips touch in an affectionate kiss.

Sabine trembles as she watches them.

They kiss again, a deeper kiss, mouth working against mouth, one body swaying against the other in the red light of the lamps.

Marthe laughs.

"I like kissing you after you've been sucking me."

Hector's hand holds one of her full breasts. Marthe fills her hand with his organ and testicles. Hector holds a breast with one hand and fondles her bottom with the other hand. They watch each other in the mirror. They watch their hands, Marthe's hand holding his organ, Hector's fingers now inside her sex. They sway against each other, their eyes on the mirror, watching the mirror as they fondle each other.

Marthe slowly pulls Hector towards the divan where Sabine pretends to sleep.

Sabine trembles.

Her aunt and uncle move past the divan to the bed. They pass so close to Sabine.

Marthe stretches out on her back. Hector straddles her and shifts his body forward and Marthe murmurs something and takes his organ in her mouth.

Marthe's lips are stretched by the girth of Hector's organ. She rubs her sex with one hand while she sucks his penis. Her sex is wet, her fingers in the wet of her sex.

Sabine can see the wetness on the fingers of her aunt.

Sabine watches everything, her eyes fixed now, her eyes mesmerized. She's afraid to move. She remains as motionless as possible, aware of everything touching her body, the sheet, the divan, aware of each heartbeat in her chest.

Hector pulls back. His organ throbs and sways as he moves back.

Marthe opens her thighs wide to him. She slides her hands along the insides of her thighs to frame the dark forest that covers her sex.

"Hurry," Marthe says with a laugh.

Hector mounts her, one hand guiding his organ, his affair pushing and entering the hairy cave, Marthe grunting with satisfaction as she feels the spearing.

They both groan, Hector and Marthe groaning in the red light of the lamps.

"Yes, it's good," Marthe says.

Her hands grip his shoulders. She holds Hector's shoulders as he begins thrusting like a stallion.

Sabine is overwhelmed. She closed her eyes. She hears the bed creaking. The bed is so close to the divan. But the urge to watch them is too strong and she wants to open her eyes again.

Suddenly Sabine feels a hand sliding under the sheet that covers her. Fingers caress her thighs, then between her thighs. The hand slides back and forth over the insides of Sabine's thighs.

Sabine's eyes are still closed. Her body is frozen into immobility. Then she hears the voice of her aunt, her aunt whispering.

"Are you sleeping? You're not sleeping, are you?"

Sabine hears the amusement in Marthe's voice.

Marthe's hand moves to cover Sabine's sex. Sabine shudders as she feels her aunt's fingers.

Marthe laughs.

"She's burning. Our darling is burning, Hector."

Sabine shudders.

Marthe pulls the sheet away and Sabine is uncovered. Then Marthe's hands pull at Sabine's nightgown, pulling at the cotton until Sabine's thighs and belly are exposed.

Hector moves behind his wife.

Marthe leans over to put her mouth on Sabine's sex.

Sabine groans as she feels her aunt's lips and then her aunt's tongue.

Marthe's probing tongue.

Sabine opens her thighs further. She pushes her pelvis upward to get more of Marthe's mouth.

But in a moment Marthe pulls her face away.

"Hector, she's a darling. Look how wet she is, how eager for it."

Sabine is vanquished.

She hears the beating of her heart again.

She opens her eyes when she feels Marthe's mouth on her sex again.

Sabine sees Hector behind Marthe, Hector thrusting in Marthe while Marthe is busy with Sabine.

The divan shakes each time Hector pushes forward.

Marthe pulls away.

"Enough. Now come into bed with us."

Her lips are wet. Marthe smiles at Sabine as Sabine stares at her aunt's wet lips.

Sabine joins them, gliding from the divan to the bed and then stretching out between them. In a moment Marthe rolls over to lie on top of Sabine, rubbing her sex against Sabine's sex, laughing against Sabine's ear as she strokes Sabine's body with her hands.

"Hector, look how beautiful she is. Look at this. These nipples. This belly. And this. How pretty it is."

Sabine's thighs are spread wide, held apart by Marthe as Hector gazes at Sabine's sex.

Her sex exposed to their eyes.

Sabine is overwhelmed, burning with

excitement.

Marthe kisses Sabine and Sabine shudders as she feels her aunt's wet mount on her lips.

She feels Hector's hands on her legs, pushing her legs upwards, pushing at her knees.

Then his organ pushing inside her sex.

Marthe laughing.

"More, Hector, with more force. Don't be a coward. She adores it. Can't you see she adores it?"

Sabine shudders as Marthe laughs again.

Laughing, laughing. Why is she laughing?

Chapter Six

*

This is the City of Kings.

Sabine and Leon are in Lima and the sun is blazing down like a beacon of paradise.

What can be wrong with such an afternoon?

They walk around the Plaza de Armas in front of the cathedral.

Leon prattles about the history of Peru. In his hands he holds the little guide-book. He mumbles something about Pizarro and Sabine looks at him.

"What?"

"Lima was founded by Pizarro."

Sabine has no idea who this Pizarro is, a name like all the other names, a sound that stirs vague memories of her childhood. She's aware of the glances of Peruvian men, their bold eyes.

Then she feels insecure again, ill at ease about her prospects. Once again she feels annoyance at Leon. Why is she a woman beset with difficulties in this place at the edge of the world?

And now suddenly Sabine sees Jimenez on the other side of the square, Señor Fernando Jimenez standing in front of the cathedral and looking at them.

Sabine quivers as she thinks of the little diplomat with his collar and his leash.

Jimenez is certainly looking at Sabine and Leon. Has he been following them? Sabine tells herself these Chileans are capable of intense jealousies and protracted madness.

"Let's make a tour of that museum," Sabine says.

"What?"

"That museum, Leon. You're not blind, are you?"

That awful building.

The bored guard at the door mumbles something and Leon hurries to find the necessary coins in his pocket. They walk inside and Sabine is grateful that at least the place is cool.

Statues in the corridors, ugly statues of dead heroes. And everywhere a smell of fresh sawdust.

But at least the place is cool.

Jimenez follows them into the museum.

Sabine hears Jimenez shouting something at the guard. Sabine's pointed heels make a clicking sound on the wooden floor as she takes Leon's arm and hurries him into one of the exhibition rooms.

And now what's this?

"Bolivar," Leon says. "Everything here is Bolivar."

An entire room devoted to Bolivar.

Leon begins reading from his guide-book again. Sabine continues holding Leon's arm but she keeps her eyes on the door to make certain that Jimenez doesn't dare enter.

When Jimenez arrives at the entrance to the Bolivar room, his eyes meet Sabine's and he blushes.

He backs away.

Sabine holds his gaze, her eyes pouring a liquid fire as she forces Jimenez to back away.

That stupid little fool.

Sabine wanders with Leon from room to room, all these portraits of bemused men with their moustaches and dark eyes, until finally she finds the exit and she pushes Leon out of the museum and into the square again.

"Enough," she says. All that horrible history.

She wants desperately to avoid that little man Jimenez. Sabine is certain that Jimenez is capable of mischief. Once again she quivers as she remembers his grovelling.

"A restaurant, Leon."

"Is it necessary?"

"It will do you some good."

Hesitant, Leon allows himself to be led into a restaurant with a large canopy over the entrance and a pair of huge ugly plants guarding the vestibule.

Well, it's Peruvian, Sabine thinks. It's the edge of the world.

The edge of the world it might be, but inside the restaurant they find a party of Germans from the ship.

One dozen of the best of the Rhineland occupy a large table surrounded by a group of perplexed Peruvian waiters.

Sabine and Leon are shown to a small table in an alcove.

"The Nazis," Leon says.

But Sabine is thankful that Jimenez is gone. She tells herself Jimenez wouldn't dare follow them into this restaurant. If one must choose between the Nazis and Jimenez, then one choose the Nazis. Well, I'm not political, Sabine thinks.

My grandmother on my mother's side was an Alsatian.

"I'm not hungry," Leon says.

Sabine frowns.

"I'd like some wine."

Leon orders a bottle of wine and a bowl of fruit. Sabine sips the wine and then she stares at the leaves of the plant behind Leon's head. She ignores the Germans. The Rhinelanders seem to be in the midst of a celebration, laughing together and maybe about to burst into a song or two.

Then suddenly Sabine senses a presence beside the table. One of the Germans. He clicks his heels and bows his head.

"We recognize you as fellow passengers. Please join us at our table."

Sabine nods.

"Yes, why not? How kind of you to invite us."

Leon makes a sound in his throat, but the German is already pulling out Sabine's chair, helping her to rise.

Sabine knows what Leon is thinking. All Nazis. But she tells herself it's a diversion. One must have an occasional diversion.

They meet the Germans. Four men and two women, all the men with noble foreheads and the women with powdered faces.

Sabine meets Gustav and Beatrix Eis.

"Delighted to meet you," Herr Eis says.

The blonde wife is cold, a smile and a nod and the blue eyes like the ice in the Baltic in January.

Sabine sits at the left hand of Gustav Eis and she listens to the chatter about the ship, the ocean, the city of Lima and the prospects for a calm voyage.

Are the Germans amused?

Gustav Eis seems to have an interest in Sabine. He smiles at her, his eyes on her throat, the light gleaming on his noble Teutonic forehead.

And Sabine is impressed. She imagines Herr Eis with his wife. That blonde blue-eyed iceberg. Does she sing like a Valkyrie when Gustav has her in the throes of passion?

Leon appears to be miserable. He says nothing, his eyes darting right and left like a cornered rat hunting for an escape. He listens as Gustav Eis talks of Peru and Pizarro and the New Order in Germany.

Then Herr Eis turns the subject to France and French women. Parisian women.

"The wisest women in the world," Herr Eis says. "Wisdom is so necessary."

Sabine accepts the compliment.

What sort of wisdom?

Sabine's interest in Herr Eis increases.

This man is someone important.

*

When Sabine and Leon finally leave the Germans and the restaurant, Jimenez is gone. The streets are quiet, nothing but yellow dust in the road in the waning light of the afternoon.

"Now you'll have your present," Sabine says.

"My present?"

"A girl, Leon. I promised you a girl."

He makes a sound of protest.

Sabine teases him.

He demurs at first but Sabine insists. He finally

agrees. As he thinks of it now, his interest is evident.

"I suppose I ought to have something."

"You deserve it."

"Yes I do. I'm a dying man and I ought to have something."

They stroll through the quarter near the cathedral, Sabine with her eyes open for a girl. She wants a girl with dark eyes for Leon, one of those Peruvian girls with a haunted look in her face.

In front of an open coffee bar, Sabine finally sees a suitable creature.

"That one, Leon?"

"Mmmm, yes."

"What marvelous hips she has."

Sabine approaches the young woman. The girl has full red lips and dark eyes and long dark hair knotted in a single braid.

"Ten soles," the girl says. "Twenty soles for two."

She agrees to go with Sabine and Leon to a hotel. She explains it will be another ten soles for the hotel room. Sabine gazes at the aggressive thrust of the girl's breasts in her blouse. She looks down to gauge the curve of the girl's derriére. How much is that in francs? Don't be silly, never mind, Sabine thinks. This is Peru and the girl is lovely.

Indeed lovely.

The girl's name is Carlita and she leads them to a small hotel squeezed between a bank and a mortuary. Sabine has a turn when she sees the name of the place: Hotel Leon.

"Look, Leon."

"What?"

"The name of the hotel."

"My God."

The trio enters. Leon pays the ten soles at the counter. The old clerk blows his nose and returns to his battered magazine.

Inside the small room, Sabine sits near the window. She decides that Carlita can't be more than eighteen. A child. An infant with impressive breasts and an aggressive behind.

"Tell me your name again," Leon says.

The girls laughs.

"Carlita."

Her name rolls out, her full red lips an enticement.

Carlita undresses as they watch her, her hips wriggling as first the tight red dress and then the red brassiere and finally the black drawers are peeled away to unveil her commodities.

Her breasts are like large pears, the dark nipples thrusting upwards and to each side. The hair on her mount is jet black and dense enough to hide any evidence of a sex. Her legs and thighs are muscular and look as firm as the bronze of one of Rodin's statues.

And her buttocks. Carlita's buttocks. What a glorious bottom she has. Leon's face shows his happiness.

Sabine tells Leon to undress.

"Hurry, darling."

Leon hurries. His face is flushed now. The girl smiles, one hand idly holding a full breast, her eyes on Leon as she estimates his intentions.

Finally Leon is naked, wearing nothing but his brown silk socks, his organ erect and bobbing as he chuckles and moves to the girl.

Leon fondles Carlita as she stands and waits. His fingers squeeze her breasts, her thighs, her buttocks.

"She's wonderful," Leon says. "What an exquisite girl."

And an accomplished girl, a girl with a clever understanding. She touches Leon's organ, draws her fingertips over his penis and down underneath to the weight of his testicles.

Leon shudders as Carlita sinks to her knees.

Her full red lips close over the tip of his organ.

Sabine sits near the window with her legs crossed as she watches it. Like the blowing of a trumpet, she thinks. Or perhaps an oboe. The sound that comes out of Leon's throat is more like the sound of an oboe.

Carlita's head bobs back and forth as she makes her music.

Then the girl pulls her mouth away and she laughs at Leon and she nods at the bed as she grips his testicles with her hand.

"The bed is better, no?"

"Yes," Leon says.

The girls looks at Sabine.

"And you, señora? Would you like me to undress you?"

Sabine is amused.

"Only the gentlemen, darling. It's him you want and not me."

The girl shrugs and looks at Leon.

"How do you want me?".

Leon pats her bottom.

"I want this."

She smiles at him and then she turns and she climbs onto the bed with her rump in the air.

The girl wriggles her bottom at Leon and Leon groans.

"Ten more soles," the girls says.

"What?"

"Ten more soles for the culo."

Sabine finds a note in her purse and she brings it to the girl.

Carlita holds the crumpled money in her hand as she wriggles her bottom again.

"I'm ready, señor."

Leon mounts her.

Sabine sits near them on the bed and she watches them.

How remarkable it is that for a brief moment Leon suddenly becomes a stallion.

The girl grunts as Leon's organ stretches her fundament.

Sabine reaches out to fondle one of Carlita's hanging breasts.

Leon pumps like an animal and he finishes quickly.

Carlita falls forward to free herself. Then she crawls away and she hurries to be dressed again.

Carlita looks bored now. She smiles at them, but the smile is unfinished as she turns to walk out of the room.

Sabine also turns; she turns to stroll to the window.

"Put your clothes on," Sabine says to Leon.

She looks at the window. At the grime. The

window is so grimy the outside world is only the vaguest blur in the distance.

*

What sort of peace is there?

Sabine dreams.

Is it Gustav Eis?

Sabine is on the stage of an empty theater, empty but for the people on the stage who are all facing in the same direction.

In front of Sabine a man is seated on a chair. She can see only the back of his head, his shoulders, his white shirt. He has his left hand raised and his forefinger is pointing upward.

To the right of the man is seated a woman: the back of a black dress, a white neck and a head of dark hair.

Sabine.

Sabine is looking at her own neck.

To the right of the woman is a small table, just a table, no chairs, and on the top of the table is a pitcher and two teacups; but the pitcher is one of those usually used for water and Sabine has no idea why the teacups are there.

The man continues to look straight ahead and point his finger upward; or perhaps his eyes are closed; Sabine can see only the back of his head and she has no way of knowing.

"Not to be expected," the man says.

Sabine, or this woman who appears to be Sabine and who sits beside the man, Sabine turns to the man, hesitates as though changing her mind, and then she turns to face the other direction.

"I don't know," Sabine says.

The voice is obviously the voice of Sabine.

Suddenly now she stands up and she walks a few steps forward and she stops. Her hands are now raised in front of her body, together perhaps, it's not possible to see, Sabine can see no more than her own back.

But not it's clear that the other Sabine, the one who is standing, is unbuttoning her dress. The style of the dress is obsolete and much too ordinary for Sabine's taste. The standing Sabine lowers each shoulder, wriggles her shoulders as the dress slides to the floor. She steps out of the fallen dress and she pushes it to the side with her left shoe. Her hands loose at her sides, she stands a moment without moving: dark hair, pink skin, a black brocade corset with lace-edge suspenders to hold up her black stockings, grey suede shoes each with a pointed heel behind and a black satin bow in front.

The legs are lovely, Sabine thinks.

She admires the bulge of her plump thighs above the tops of her dark stockings.

Now abruptly the Sabine who is standing removes everything in rapid sequence: the shoes, the stockings ungartered and peeled away, the corset, the drawers under the corset, everything away, everything tossed to the floor on top of the dress, and then once again she stands erect with her hands loose at her sides, her body naked now, her skin pink and tender in the soft light.

The man in the white shirt still has his left hand raised and his forefinger pointing upward.

The Sabine who is standing finally moves her

right hand. She fondles a wobbly buttock, pulls it up and lets it fall again.

"Everything these days is difficult," she says.

The man in the white shirt now lowers his raised forefinger. He rises up and he advances toward the standing Sabine, comes up behind her, halts, places a hand on each of her buttocks, vigorously kneads and squeezes her flesh.

"Excellent," he says. "We'll have another try tomorrow."

Sabine moves away from his hands and the hands are clutching at empty space.

"You don't understand," she says.

She turns. She struts back to the chair and she sits down and now once again the first Sabine is staring at the back of her own neck.

But is it Gustav Eis?

*

The ship's doctor is unhappy.

Arthur Gordon does not look at all happy. He looks unhealthy. It occurs to Sabine that a member of the medical profession ought to be more robust.

"You don't look well," she says.

Doctor Gordon turns his sad eyes away as the breeze ruffles his hair. The ship is sailing north now, past Peru and Ecuador and on to Panama.

Now Doctor Gordon looks at Sabine again, his discomfort evident in his slack lips.

"That Jimenez fellow is not what you think."

"And what do I think?"

"He's not all that rich. The purser says Jimenez hasn't much in the way of anything."

"But he's a diplomat."

"Yes, I suppose you might call it that."

And so Doctor Gordon gives his report. Jimenez is something of a *poseur*. A wife with the look of a washerwoman, according to the pursuer, who happened to have seen the wife in Valparaiso.

Señor Jimenez is a man who hangs on.

"Well, I'm not surprised," Sabine says.

"You said he was rich."

"I said nothing of the kind."

"In any case, what does it matter?"

"I want you to find out about someone else."

Doctor Gordon groans.

"Who is it now?"

"A German gentleman. His name is Gustav Eis. Do you know him?"

"Sabine, I refuse. It's awful."

"You'll do it, won't you, darling?"

"Are you a spy of some sort? I don't want any political difficulties."

Sabine is amused.

"You're a fool, aren't you?"

The doctor flushes, his thin face going red as his eyes come to rest on the swell of Sabine's breasts in her white blouse.

Sabine inclines her head. She still has the power over Doctor Gordon and it's only a question of time before he settles down again.

"I don't like the Germans," Doctor Gordon says.

Sabine touches his hand.

"You'll find out what you can, won't you, darling?"

He finally agrees. His face is so pink in the afternoon light. He will make inquiries about the German Gustav Eis. And the wife too. The blue-eyed Frau Beatrix Eis.

When Doctor Gordon leaves her, Sabine turns to look at a pair of sailors on the deck. Not the one who had her that time. But do they know? She wonders if the sailors talk. For a moment she wants these two. She imagines having them both; she imagines herself between a pair of apes.

But she controls herself. She cautions herself with a quiet shudder. She needs to devote her energies to finding a new benefactor. One must apply reason to one's existence. The sailors can wait. Sabine, darling, hold the apes in abeyance.

*

Señor Jimenez trembles as he holds his brandy in the salon. His eyes are so meek.

"I beg you, Sabine."

"Definitely not."

"I'll kill myself and you'll be responsible for it."

"I don't care what you do, I won't see you any more."

Sabine refuses to look at him now. She taps her knee with irritation, her eyes on the men at the bar, the two card tables, the empty writing desk against the far wall. It's not much of a salon, is it? What an awful ship this is.

Jimenez whines. He begs her.

"You can command any favor from me."

"Don't be a fool."

He whispers at her:

"I'm your slave."

"My little piggy."

"Yes."

A shudder of delight passes through her as she remembers his collar.

"You're an idiot."

He begs again, his voice whining and panic in his eyes.

"I'll do anything you want."

"I'll think about it."

Well, he might be useful somehow.

*

Champagne on the evening of the 27th of April.

A crowd in the salon. The captain stands on a dais, his face pink, his glass raised, his lips working beneath his red moustache as he forms the words of a toast.

"To the equator. The H.M.S. Reina del Pacifico is about to cross the equatorial latitude into the northern hemisphere."

Sabine and Leon are seated at a table. Sabine wears a white evening dress with large balloon sleeves. She sits back a bit from the table, her legs crossed, her right hand on her right knee, her left hand at her side with her fingers extended along her left thigh. Her head is inclined slightly to the right and she looks pensive.

Leon sits opposite Sabine at the table, sitting back in his chair, sitting there in evening dress with a red carnation attached to the left lapel of his jacket, a white silk handkerchief extended precisely two inches out of the breast pocket of his jacket, his eyes on Sabine, his face not at all happy.

They do not face each other. Sabine is looking at the crowd and Leon has his eyes fixed on Sabine.

On the table is a floral centerpiece, one glass of champagne in front of Sabine and one glass of champagne in front of Leon.

The bottle of champagne, if it still exists, is nowhere to be seen.

Between Sabine and Leon stands a waiter, a man in a short white jacket, a bald head, his two hands holding a silver tray, a white towel fastened to a catch of some sort at his belt.

On the silver tray is a single packet of cigarettes and a box of matches.

And the crowd? And the others in the crowd?

The ship's doctor Arthur Gordon is at the edge of the crowded floor with an English couple named Selby. Nora Selby has a cigarette in her mouth and Gordon is at Nora's left and leaning forward with a lighted match in his hand. Anthony Selby, Nora's husband, stands at Nora's right with his hands in his pockets and his eyes on the lighted match.

And across the floor some sixty feet away is Señor Fernando Jimenez with an Italian couple, the couple seen so often by Sabine on deck, Signor Vincente Forli and his wife Lucia, the wife so thin in a black evening dress, leaning forward of course with a cigarette in her mouth, leaning forward to have the cigarette lighted by the gold lighter in the hand of Jimenez.

Lucia Forli has closed her gloved hand over the

hand of Jimenez as he holds the cigarette lighter. Signor Forli stands between them with a benign look as he watches the process.

And the Germans? It's useless to count the Germans on the passenger list, or the Germans in the salon on the evening of the 27th of April in the year 1936, this evening of champagne as the H.M.S. Reina del Pacífico begins its passage across the equatorial latitude.

Three Germans at least. At the far end of the salon, Beatrix Eis stands with a man on either side of her. One man is Gustav Eis and he stands at her left with his head thrown back and his face in the midst of a hearty laugh. The other man is not laughing, but his lips are turned in a smile. Beatrix Eis herself is laughing, but the laugh is more restrained than her husband's, a spreading of her rouged lips, the spread wide enough to show her white teeth, but nothing else is displaced and certainly her head is not thrown back like the head of her husband.

The captain announces the crossing of the equator and the crowd cheers.

Leon is unhappy as he pays ten francs for the packet of cigarettes. He leans forward to offer a cigarette to Sabine but she refuses.

Arthur Gordon finishes lighting the cigarette of Nora Selby whie Nora's husband watches them.

Fernando Jimenez finishes lighting the cigarette of Lucia Forli while Lucia's husband watches them.

The Germans continue laughing.

At ten minutes before midnight, Leon leaves the salon and Arthur Gordon approaches the table where Sabine is still seated.

"That German you wanted to know about."

Sabine looks up at him.

"Yes?"

"It seems he owns a large piece of Berlin."

Someone is playing a piano now. A young lad,
at the piano is in the midst of singing an English
song. Sabine turns her head to look at the group
of Germans, to gaze at the profile of Gustav Eis.

Well, they do have boulevards, don't they? Berlin isn't Paris, but they do have boulevards.

Chapter Seven

*

Sabine is frightened by old age.

She imagines herself wrinkled and bent, an old woman with a resemblance to a statue. And here is the old woman bending her knees. Sabine wonders if she'll be in one piece at the end. Will she still have her figure? Or will she appear like those women one sees in the markets: the upholstery bulging everywhere through the dull cotton covering?

I'll be an old woman who spends the evening talking. I'll talk about matters of no significance.

Then she tells herself to stop thinking about it. She will not allow herself to think about it. She resolves to control her attitudes. She sits in a chair and she crosses her legs. Such a small pleasure it is and yet so perfect. She does it again now, the left leg over the right leg. Then right over left. She adores the slowness of it, the careful arrangement, the rubbing of her silk stockings. She adores the way the excitement builds under the long skirt as she continues the rhythmic flexing of her thighs. With amusement she recalls an occasion in a crowded drawing room when she reached a crisis without ceasing to speak to her friends.

I do not pretend to an excessive modesty.

Sabine thinks about the English doctor. Does she treat him unfairly? He's always worried about something or other, always with a furrowed brow. She remembers that minister Daurez; yes, Doctor Gordon reminds her of Daurez. Different coloring, of course, but the same type. At least the English doctor claims to be nothing but an ordinary man. You must be kind to him, Sabine thinks. The bonbons must be parcelled out. She tells herself not to be concerned about all the petty annoyances that occur on this ship.

Then she feels a sudden terror again as she remembers that Leon may indeed be dying. She thinks of all the humiliations that might await her in Paris. You must conquer it, she thinks. You must never use the wrong voice. She thinks of Doctor Gordon's eyes. His skin is so pink. She thinks of his blonde hair as he bends to suck at her sex. My English cavalier.

Now from somewhere comes the odor of flowers. Sabine imagines herself in a church in the south of France. She finds a dark niche and she stands there a moment with her buttocks pushing against the stone wall. She sways her hips from side to side to get the feel of the cool stone against the cheeks of her bottom. Sabine, you're a profane creature. But what an extreme annoyance it is to be deprived of her pleasures.

Is my soul damned? My sex is open. In the presence of God, my sex is open.

What she wants is a man with a kind heart. Is it the women who are vile or the men? All her acquaintances are hypocrites and imposters. She doesn't want to think of it. This love she wants, she knows it's beyond her.

What I need is a refuge. Yes, I do need that. I

ought to pray for that. I never did in Paris. In Paris she was often so concerned with passing the time. Her pleasure is putting on her clothes and then taking them off again, dressing and undressing in a slow ritual before a full-length mirror. And preferably with some puppy dog lover sitting nearby to watch her. He might sit with a prayerbook in his hands as she watches the clothing and unclothing of her body. He holds the prayer book but he doesn't take his eyes off Sabine. She adores the glint in his eyes. She smiles at him as she reveals her breasts again, as she touches her nipples.

Sabine thinks about the passengers on the Reina del Pacifico. Some of them are passing her now as she sits there in her deck chair in the shade of one of the ship's funnels. In the afternoons her pleasure is to sit alone and watch the passengers. Each group is another spectacle. The women. That brawny girl with tanned arms. Is that man the girl's uncle or the girl's lover? Or is it possible he's both? Yes, it's possible. The girl is no more than eighteen and she has pretty eyes.

*

Leon is groaning in the afternoon heat.

He has his mouth pressed against Sabine's sex. They lie on the bed and Leon's body is turned so that Sabine can hold his palpitating organ in her right hand.

Leon groans again. His tongue has stopped moving and Sabine is annoyed. He pretends to be mute and dead but the penis in her hand is throbbing.

Sabine strokes his penis with a deliberate slowness. She wants Leon to consider himself, to consider his own being. She feels his pleasure with her fingers.

Now Leon's tongue is moving again and Sabine sighs. What a miracle it is to feel a soft wet tongue caressing her clitoris. If Leon has a soul, then his soul has now moved to his tongue. He keeps his mouth open as he rubs his soul back and forth over Sabine's swollen clitoris.

He's a child, Sabine thinks. Leon is my child.

She doesn't care what others think. She looks down at his organ now. She senses him close to a crisis and she moves her fingers more rapidly. She hurries the soft skin back and forth over the knob of his organ.

Sabine watches the spurting, the gushing of Leon's milk.

Does she despise him for it?

Leon groans once more against her sex.

As Sabine's fingers complete the milking, a long shudder of divine ecstasy passes from one end of her body to the other.

Chapter Eight

*

Opportunity beckons at five degrees north.

No more than two days after the Reina del Pacifico crosses the equator, Sabine sees Gustav Eis alone on the foredeck.

A sense of urgency now. Santiago is only a memory and the reality of Europe is beckoning to Sabine. She has her chance and a woman who misses her chance is worthy only of scorn.

She arranges her dress and she waits for the moment when Gustav Eis will notice her in her chair on the deck not twenty yards from where he stands at the rail.

Finally he turns and he sees her. He immediately approaches. He clicks his heels and he bows.

"Good morning, madame."

"Good morning, Herr Eis."

"So you remember my name. I'm honored, madame."

They begin chatting. Once again Sabine is impressed by his white teeth. She invites him to sit beside her and Herr Eis immediately accepts.

"The sun is so hot in this part of the world."

"Like a ball of fire."

His interest in Sabine is obvious. She wears a white cotton dress, white silk stockings and white shoes of the softest leather. Eis gazes at her ankles. A sea bird shrieks out as it glides across the bow of the ship. Eis stares at the bird a moment and then he looks at Sabine's ankles again.

"I think I'd like to walk," Sabine says. "Would you care to come with me."

They walk together around the deck, down the starboard side and up the port side. Eis is talking about French women again, like that day in the restaurant in Lima.

Sabine teases him.

"You admire French women too much."

Eis laughs.

"I adore them."

Now a breeze molds Sabine's dress to her body and she gathers the dress with her hand to avoid losing it to the wind.

"My friend isn't feeling well."

"Your friend?"

"Monsieur Mabeuf. It seems he has a bad heart and he won't live very long."

"I'm so sorry."

"It's awful, isn't it."

"Illness is a terrible thing. And also imagined illness. Isn't that so? My poor wife refuses to leave her cabin until noon because she imagines she has an illness of some kind."

Herr Eis sighs as he talks about his wife.

Sabine sighs as she talks about Leon.

"And in the morning my poor Leon is already too exhausted to keep me company on the deck."

"Then allow me the honor of being your morning companion."

Sabine leans against the rail, her eyes on the open sea, on the far horizon.

"Yes, that's kind of you, isn't it?"

When they part he kisses her hand. Sabine turns, convinced she'll have her success with him. She drifts away with an awareness of his eyes on her back. She twitches her behind a bit; just a bit of twitching to set his mind working.

The Germans aren't so bad, are they?

Some of them know how to pine and swoon. Sabine thinks of Gustav Eis as she leaves the deck and returns to her cabin.

*

The next morning Sabine convinces Leon to remain in his bed.

"You don't look well at all. Are you feeling ill? Darling, I don't want you to be miserable. You need to conserve your strength, don't you?"

She puts rouge on her lips while Leon lies in bed with a stuporous look on his face.

Sabine goes out. She meets Eis in the dining room and they have breakfast together. It's a bright morning and Eis is cheerful, solicitous, gallant in the way he arranges the ham on her plate.

"And your friend? How is he this morning?"

"He feels awful. He's always so weak in the morning."

"Yes, weakness in a man is an unpleasant thing."

"In a woman too."

"You have lovely hair. Your hair catches the light in a certain way and it's lovely."

But his eyes are elsewhere. Herr Eis keeps his eyes on Sabine's breasts as he tells her how striking she is.

She teases him.

"You're flirting with me."

"Yes."

"But you have a wife."

"I'm afraid Beatrix is too much like your friend."

After breakfast Sabine and Eis take a turn around the deck. Sabine takes his arm and Eis shows his pleasure by covering her hand with his. Sabine feels the sense of conspiracy now. Eis has his wife and she Sabine has her Leon, and yet here they are walking on the deck together arm in arm.

When they stop at the rail, Eis once again tells her how beautiful she is.

"Your eyes are magnificent. Such exquisite French eyes."

And his eyes? Sabine sees the adoration in his eyes, the reverence so crucial to her.

Her eyes meet his.

"You make me feel strange inside."

She touches his hand with her fingers. They both look down as she covers his hand with her own.

*

In the heat of the afternoon Sabine lies beside Leon and she watches him sleep. She thinks about her blossoming little affair with Herr Eis. Careful planning is needed. She can have him if she wants him, she's certain of it. The wife is an impediment, but of course any wife is an impediment when one has an interest in the husband.

Then Sabine considers the wisdom of it. Is it prudent? She's of an age when mistakes need to be avoided. Leon was such a mistake and now she needs to be careful not to repeat it.

Then she tells herself she has no choice; Eis is her chance. She trusts Arthur Gordon. The English doctor is not a man to be deceitful. Arthur is loyal to her now. His information is accurate. I must believe him, Sabine thinks. I need someone. I need Gustav Eis. Cherbourg isn't that far now. I do want to be in Paris again. It's so awful of Leon to leave me without anything. And when will he die? He says he won't last until Cherbourg but Arthur says it's not certain. I need an apartment in Paris. Something elegant and warm enough in winter. And new clothes. Leon is a beast, isn't he? It's so thoughtless of him. I do need new clothes and I've no idea what they're wearing in Paris now.

And what if Leon discovers her affair with Eis? Of course he'll be furious. Sabine is confident. She can manage Leon. She needs to get on with it. She needs Gustav Eis. She needs to accomplish it.

Sabine watches the twitching in Leon's face as he snores in the heat beside her.

*

The next morning Sabine sees Eis again. As usual they have breakfast together in this ship's dining room. Eis is solicitous as always. Sabine notices now that his mouth is almost delicate when he smiles.

She sits with him on deck after breakfast. Is he

aware of her perfume? He talks about his travels in Argentina and he warms to her. He talks about Europe and the new politics. Sabine has no interest in any of it; she thinks only of what she needs to accomplish with Eis.

Then he places his hand on her knee and he talks about how much he loves Paris. His fingers are bony. His fingers close over her knee, rubbing at her thin dress and the stocking underneath it.

He seems hungry for her and Sabine is amused by it. She feels confident again. His eyes are on her breasts again. A sea bird is gliding over the stern again. Sabine suddenly remembers the sailor she bought, the throbbing of the engines. She's had no diversion since then. She feels her blood rising as she thinks about the sailor.

Eis pulls his hand away as he talks, and then later once again his hand is on her knee. He fondles her kneecap.

Sabine looks at his face.

"What do you want?"

Nothing shows in his eyes.

"Want?"

"Yes, what do you want from me?"

He hesitates.

"I suppose I want you."

Reverence in his eyes? Oh, yes, definitely reverence in his eyes. He's like a small boy now.

"Do you want to make love to me?"

"How wonderful the way you say that."

"Is that what you want?"

"Yes."

"Well, I'll consider the possibility of it. I won't

tell you now, but maybe tomorrow."

"You'll make me extremely happy."

"Yes of course."

*

Another sweltering day. Sabine lies alone in the heat, sprawled naked on the bed with her right hand covering her sex.

Her fingers move. She opens the groove to find her clitoris. She thinks of all the years in Paris and how so much has come to nothing. She toys with her little pearl, her fingers stroking it. Well, you're an orphan, Sabine thinks. Then she tells herself she's no longer a child and her attitudes are ridiculous. Her sex is so wet, the sap running out to cover her fingers. Sabine, you ought to be religious; you ought to find something in the church. In the meantime she holds her clitoris, the hard length of it between her fingertips. She moves it with a certain insistence, this tiny burning nub that she has. Her legs are shaking now. She turns her head to the side to avoid the bright light of the porthole. Does she still wear the mask of serenity? She groans. The hand moves with more conviction, a constant rubbing and churning of her sex. Sabine quivers and groans as the crisis approaches. She thinks of Paris, the Seine, the boats on the Seine.

A final shudder passes through the body as she pushes her face into the soft pillow.

*

In the afternoon Sabine summons Jimenez to where she sits reading on the deck under an

· 100 ·

awning.

The Chilean arrives with his face flushed, one hand wiping at his forehead with a white handkerchief.

"It's much too hot."

"You can be of some help to me now."

"Anything, my love."

"Don't call me that, you fool. Not here."

"Yes, how stupid of me."

"I want the use of your cabin in the morning. Can you arrange to be somewhere else for a few hours tomorrow morning? I want your cabin."

His eyes are puzzled.

"My cabin?"

"Yes, darling, your cabin."

"Where will I write my letters? I use the cabin to write my letters in the morning."

But of course the business is settled.

*

Sabine has dinner with Leon in the crowded dining room. They sit isolated in a corner, but now Sabine pays more attention to the doings on the other side of the large room. The Germans. Now she has more interest in the Germans. Gustav and Beatrix are having their dinner with another couple, the four people talking constantly with an air of happiness.

Happy about what?

Leon seems happy. Sabine turns away from Leon and she looks at the Germans again. Beatrix Eis is a puzzle. Sabine imagines Gustav and Beatrix together. She imagines the grunting. Gustav has the appearance of a man who grunts when he makes love. And Beatrix? Does she moan? Does she abandon herself? Once again Sabine thinks of Gustav's mouth, his pink lips. She wonders how skillful he is with his tongue. A quiver of excitement passes through Sabine. When the waiter arrives, Leon smiles at Sabine.

"Coffee, my love?"

Sabine imagines Gustav and Beatrix again. Now Beatrix is leaning forward with her hands on a bed, her fingers gripping the counterpane. Is it the cabin? The light from the porthole brings a glow to the blonde hair. Beatrix wears a white blouse, but below the waist she's naked. And Gustav is naked behind her. Beatrix arches her back to make her buttocks more prominent. Gustav has already penetrated her, his organ like a thick truncheon extending out between the cheeks of her bottom.

Which entrance is he using? Sabine contemplates the question. She decides Gustav is using the more familiar place. He has his organ stroking in the blonde sex of his wife.

Beatrix has her mouth open. Her body shakes a bit each time Gustav pushes his belly against her bottom. Gustav runs his hands over his wife's rump. Gustav is thrusting. Sabine imagines the grunting again. Gustav grunting and Beatrix moaning.

In the dining room, Leon makes a noise.

"Sabine, darling, you look so pensive."

*

Eis is nervous.

"Early this morning I saw the coast of

Columbia."

Sabine doesn't care about Columbia. She sips her coffee, amused at the way he fidgets like a schoolboy about to lose his virginity.

After breakfast they walk to the stern to look at the seagulls.

"Do you still want to make love to me?"

"Yes of course."

She leads him off the deck and into the passageway that runs to the cabins. Eis seems afraid of discovery, his eyes haunted as he peers right and left each time they cross an open space.

Then at last she has him at the door of the cabin she wants.

"In here."

"Whose cabin is it?"

"A friend. Hurry, darling."

The Chilean's cabin enfolds them as they slip inside and close the door.

Sabine allows Eis to kiss her neck. A shiver runs through her body as she feels his hot lips on her skin.

He presses against her, mumbles something into the shell of her ear. But when his fingers work at the buttons of her dress, she pushes him away.

"Not that way."

She glances down at the bulge in his trousers. And then she touches it. She fondles him through his trousers. Eis stands there motionless, his eyes on her fingers, his body frozen in his immobility.

Sabine nods.

"Well, you're in form, aren't you?"

"My darling . . ."

"You want to make me happy, don't you?"

"Yes of course."

She moves away from him. She finds the chair near the small desk at which Jimenez writes his letters. She slips her shoes off and then she sits down in the chair with her knees drawn up and her feet on the seat of the chair with her toes extending over the edge.

Today she wears no underpants, nothing under the white dress except her white stockings gartered above her knees. The dress is now pulled back and with her knees apart Eis can see everything there is to see: her legs, her thighs, her dark sex exposed to his eyes.

"Come here and suck it," she says.

He stands transfixed.

"Dear God . . ."

"Don't you want to? It's what I enjoy. If you want to make me happy, you'll do it."

"You're a witch."

"Is that what you think? Well, if you don't want to, I suppose you can leave now."

But he comes forward. He drops to his knees in front of her and in a moment his mouth presses fervently against her open sex.

Sabine strokes his head.

"That's lovely, Gustav. I like the name Gustav. It has such a sweet sound to it. Don't you think it's a sweet name? Suck a bit harder, darling. Yes, that's perfect. That's quite perfect."

Victory. His mouth is clever. She closes her eyes a moment and then she opens them again.

She keeps him at it until the spasm arrives, the tremblings in her legs and thighs, the quivering in her belly. She strokes his hair, his pink forehead, his ears. She moans softly, bites her lip to stop it as she closes her thighs against his head.

Gustav is such a lovely name.

When at last he pulls his mouth away, Sabine smiles down at him.

"Was it nice for you, Gustav? Do you like doing that?"

Sabine is thrilled as she imagines she hears the beating of his heart.

Chapter Nine

*

Well, it's not the first one is it, not the first Berliner or the first German?

In 1920 the winter in Paris is the coldest in years, dreary cold days with not a hint of sun and nothing but misery in the faces of people. In December Sabine is living in a hole in Montparnasse, a garret with a skylight that needs to be shut tight to keep out the cold air. Sabine has fled the house of her aunt and uncle. She works as a shopgirl and she lives in poverty and her future looks as empty as the cardboard suitcase she keeps under her bed in the garret.

Late one afternoon as she sits in a café on the Boulevard Raspail with a miserable coffee, Sabine is approached by a man with a jaunty hat and an orange scarf and feverish eyes. He says he's a painter. He sits down at her table. He says Sabine is the most beautiful creature he's seen in years.

"I want you to pose for me."

At first Sabine refuses to believe he's actually a painter. He looks like one of those bums that hang out on the banks of the Seine. His clothes are tattered. He seems ill, coughing constantly with that feverish look in his eyes. And he's sweating. The temperature outside is close to freezing and even inside the café it's not that warm, but this man now sitting at Sabine's table is sweating.

"Darling, will you pose for me?"

Sabine shrugs.

"I'm not a model and I have no interest in it."

His eyes are burning.

"I'll pay you, of course. You won't be doing it for nothing."

Then he talks about her beauty again. He says her face is exquisite, her lips enough to make a man melt with desire. Sabine thinks he's crazy. He begs her. He offers her more money. Is he truly an artist? The coat he wears looks like a rag.

But she finally agrees. She tells herself it's a diversion and a chance to earn some money. She does need the money. With a few francs she might get herself some decent clothes to wear.

Sabine leaves the café with the painter and he leads her along the Boulevard Raspail to another place where he wants to meet some of his friends. Yes, he does have friends. In the second café everyone seems to know him. They call him Modi. There's a great deal of backslapping and Sabine tells herself that at least her painter is authentic.

He borrows money from his friends to pay Sabine. Then he leads her out of the café and he hurries her along the streets to his studio. He's drunker than ever now, drunk and coughing and talking constantly about the wonderful picture he's going to paint. He continues raving about her beauty. He says he'll make her immortal. He says everyone in the world will know about her beauty as soon as he finishes her portrait.

Sabine knows nothing about art. His name is

Modi, but for all she knows his name might be Michelangelo. Is it true that most painters are crazy? Well, this one is certainly like a wild lunatic.

His studio in the Rue de la Grande Chaumiere is a hovel, the air filled with a smell of paint and oil and hardly any furniture in the place except for a few chairs and a messy worktable under a glass roof. The disorder, the rags on the floor, the streaks of paint on the walls, the broken pottery in a corner, the look of complete dishevelment frightens Sabine and now she changes her mind and she wants to leave.

Modi begs her.

"Please, darling, don't abandon me."

He coughs again. His eyes are so red. He waves his hands in the air as he begs her stay and pose for him.

She stays.

When she takes her clothes off, he becomes ecstatic. He begins ranting again, talking about the light on her skin, the color. He lights another lamp, moves it right and left until he has the light the way he wants it.

Sabine enjoys exhibiting herself. She watches his eyes, wondering what he sees. Is it true that a painter looks at the body of a woman without passion? He's too drunk. He's a lunatic and his eyes show nothing. She says she's cold and Modi hurries to light the stove.

He poses her lying on her side with a group of pillows.

"You're an odalisque," he says.

"What's that?"

"A Turkish concubine."

"But I'm not Turkish, I'm French."

He talks constantly about her beauty, the beauty of her body, her face, her breasts, her belly. Sabine wonders if he wants to make love to her. She wouldn't mind it. As crazy as he is, he's handsome.

Finally he begins painting her. Now he shows only fierce concentration. He stops only to drink more wine out of an open bottle, raising the bottle to his lips and then wiping his mouth with his sleeve. When she tells him he drinks too much, he says he's going to die soon and it doesn't matter. He laughs at something and then his voice becomes mournful and he begins singing in a strange language.

"Yisgaddal v'yiskaddash sh'neh rabbo . . ."

"What are you singing?"

"A prayer for the dead."

Now Sabine is frightened again. A shudder of fear passes through her as she watches him work so fiercely at the canvas.

Suddenly someone is pounding at the door and the next moment the door opens and a visitor arrives.

Sabine hurries to cover herself. Modi shouts at the visitor, waving his arms and ordering him out. The visitor, a plump man in a heavy brown coat and a brown felt hat, pleads with Modi, talks about buying his paintings, talks about money. In any case they know each other and before long Modi has calmed down and the visitor sits down.

Modi introduces the visitor: a German named Kleiber, an art collector and dealer living in

Paris.

But Sabine refuses to pose anymore.

Kleiber begs Sabine to continue posing. He offers to double her fee.

Sabine thinks of the clothes she wants to buy. She decides to ignore Kleiber. She decides to ignore his leering eyes. She nods and she uncovers her body again so that Modi can continue painting.

Kleiber talks. Modi continues drinking and painting, ignoring Kleiber, mumbling something when Kleiber asks a question.

But Kleiber's eyes are always on Sabine. She can feel his eyes. She decides it's not that bad. She has pretty breasts and it's not that bad.

"Well, it's finished," Modi says.

He throws the palette knife down and he raises the wine bottle to his lips again.

"It's a masterpiece," Kleiber says.

"Pay her, you bastard."

Sabine hurries to get herself dressed again. When Kleiber pays her, he leers at her with his eyes on her breasts.

"You're the most beautiful model in Paris."

Sabine looks at the painting of herself and she thinks it's amusing. The girl in the painting has such a dead expression, such empty eyes.

Kleiber wants to buy the painting but Modi refuses.

"Talk to Zborowski."

"The hell with Zborowski. I'll pay you more than Zborowski will."

"Not this painting, you ass. Leave me alone."

Modi lies down on an old sofa near the wall

and he passes out drunk.

Sabine leaves the studio with Kleiber.

"Come with me," Kleiber says.

"To where?"

"My apartment, of course."

He hails a taxi. Sabine decides it's better than her garret. Kleiber's coat is of the purest wool and it must cost as much as she earns in a month.

In the taxi he fondles her. Sabine remains passive, her eyes on the wet streets as Kleiber's plump hands move over her legs and thighs.

He takes her to an apartment in the Rue Madeleine. Sabine is impressed. Kleiber lives in luxury, deep carpets, silk paper on the walls, the furniture covered with velvet and brocade.

"Do you like it?"

"Yes, it's lovely," Sabine says.

"This is where you belong, not with that stupid bohemian."

Kleiber talks constantly, his fingers waving at her. He tells her the painter Modi is an Italian Jew named Modigliani. Sabine doesn't care one way or the other. She's fascinated by Kleiber's collection of jewelled boxes.

"He's hanging on too long," Kleiber says.

"Who is?"

"Our friend Modigliani. It doesn't do the galleries any good, you know. Of course he'll drink himself to death, but he'd better do it quickly. What these artists need to do is work like hell and then die as quickly as possible. Modi is just hanging on and making difficulties for everyone. They're all alike, aren't they? Fools and drunkards. Are you hungry, darling? I'll have the maid bring something for you."

Now Kleiber gets amorous again. He talks about Sabine's body. He runs his hands over her shoulders and across her breasts. He giggles as he squeezes one of her breasts through her clothes with his fat fingers.

"I can't resist you," he says. "I'm completely in your power."

Then the maid arrives with food and wine. Sabine can see the maid disapproves of her. Sabine imagines the elegant women who visit this apartment. The maid would rather serve an elegant lady with jewels at her throat.

When the maid leaves, Kleiber has Sabine sit on the sofa beside him. He opens her dress and he bares her shoulders. He pulls the dress down to expose her breasts. He kisses Sabine's breasts with his wet mouth, his lips making her shudder as they pull at her nipples.

Then he gets down on the floor and he begins kissing her knees. Sabine gazes at him, watching him as he makes love to her legs. She watches his lips as he kisses the silk of her stockings.

She suddenly understands. She understands Kleiber. An instinctual understanding takes possession of her.

She looks around her. She finds the luxury in his apartment impressive. The opulence is more than she's ever seen. Everything is so soft and comfortable, everything clean and smelling of nothing but sweetness.

Sabine decides she wants to live with Kleiber. The thought of returning to her garret makes her tremble with dismay.

Kleiber looks up at her.

"Do you like it when I kiss your legs?"

"Yes."

"You can kick me if you want."

"What?"

"Kick me, darling. Go on, kick me."

She does it. She kicks his shoulder with her foot. And then she does it again.

"Is that what you want?"

Kleiber groans, his face red, his wet lips working one over the other.

"Yes."

"Kiss my shoe."

He kisses the toe of her shoe. When he tries to kiss her ankle, she pulls her foot away.

"You must beg for it."

He groans again.

"Please, darling . . ."

She has it now. She has the knowing of it.

"You're a fat worm, aren't you?"

A squeal comes out of his throat.

"Yes."

"Well, get your clothes off and we'll see."

On his knees on the carpet, Kleiber hurries to get himself naked. He works in a frenzy, as though frightened that she might change her mind and tell him to stop.

When he's naked, he kneels on the carpet on all fours, his plump body pink in the lamplight, his penis and testicles almost hidden by the hang of his belly.

"What's that? What's that around your neck?"

Kleiber touches the gold chain.

"A cross. It belonged to my mother."

A shudder runs through Sabine. She slips her shoes off. She calmly pulls her dress back and she begins unrolling her stockings. She undresses as she sits on the sofa, her clothes dropped to the side to hang over one of the arms.

Kleiber's mouth hangs open as he watches her.

When Sabine is naked, she settles herself again and she opens her thighs.

"All right, suck me off, you beast."

A sound of happiness comes out of Kleiber's throat as he scurries forward to do her bidding.

She hates it. At first she finds him disgusting. But then soon she begins to like it. At least he's ardent. She does nothing except watch him feed at her trough. She likes the laziness of it.

During the next hour Sabine cleverly masters Kleiber. She learns he will do anything she wants. She makes him crawl over the carpet, the gold cross dangling from his neck, dangling and swinging back and forth as he crawls. She taunts him about his body, the plump softness of his flesh, his limp organ.

"Don't you ever get hard?"

"Only sometimes."

"And when is that?"

He brings her a piece of black velvet and he says if she rubs his penis with it he'll soon have an erection.

Sabine is amused. His testicles remind her of Uncle Hector. Such fat pink balls. But Kleiber's penis hangs like a deflated sausage and it's not at all like Uncle Hector's.

She takes the square of black velvet and she rubs Kleiber's organ with it.

The great miracle occurs, the rising of the phoenix, the pink sausage swelling up like a balloon beneath Sabine's fingers.

He's groaning now, and as the velvet continues rubbing over his penis he makes a sudden croaking sound as the end arrives.

Sabine watches the ejaculation with curiosity, her fingers holding his penis as the milky fluid gushes out.

"Dear God," Kleiber says.

When she finally exhausts him, he begs her to move in with him. He says his life means nothing without her.

"I'll be your slave."

"The maid doesn't like me."

"Heavens, I'll sack the maid. I won't let you go."

So there it is. Sabine quits her job and she moves in with Kleiber to become his mistress.

She feels no disgust with him any more. She finds him amusing now. He's like a toy, always at her feet, always sucking her sex when she wishes it. He buys her new clothes. He takes her to the cafés and bistros and she enjoys his money. He seems to know everyone in Paris. Does anyone like him? Sabine doesn't care what anyone thinks about him.

A few weeks after Sabine begins living with Kleiber, the painter Modigliani dies.

Kleiber owns a dozen of the Italian's paintings and he expects to make a fortune.

"I'll make a pile," Kleiber says. "And if I hold out there'll be even more."

Three days later a thousand people go to the

Italian's funeral and burial in Pere-Lachaise Cemetery.

Including Kleiber. He goes to the funeral along with the others. He wants Sabine to go but she refuses.

"The painters are so boring," Sabine says.

She's had enough of them in all the cafés she's frequented with Kleiber. Sabine remains at home to enjoy the luxury of Kleiber's apartment. She drinks tea and then after that she polishes her fingernails. She talks to the new maid about the clothes she wants for the evening.

When Kleiber returns from the funeral, he carries a painting with him. He laughs as he unwraps the painting in the drawing room. Kleiber has bought Modigliani's painting of Sabine.

"Look at it," Kleiber says.

Sabine looks. She sees herself in the pose of a Turkish courtesan.

"I want you like that," Kleiber says. "Will you do it? Will you pose for me?"

Sabine humors him. She removes all her clothes. She poses on the divan like an odalisque. Kleiber is in a rapture. He falls to his knees and he begins kissing her toes. He kisses her legs and thighs. He kisses Sabine's buttocks, wet kisses covering the ivory skin of each cheek. Sabine quivers as she rolls over on her belly. Kleiber makes a sound of pleasure as he pushes his face between the firm globes of Sabine's behind. Then he begins a *feuille de rose,* his tongue like an agile serpent in Sabine's bottomhole.

Sabine quivers as she stares at the painting of herself. No, she doesn't like the painting. It's awful. The empty eyes make her look so dead.

Chapter Ten

*

The Germans have gathered on the deck of the Reina del Pacifico and the French and the English are uneasy.

The Rhinelanders make their amusements, a series of games, a bursting into song as they raise their arms to the sky. Leon refuses to watch it. He leaves Sabine and she sits on the deck with her eyes on the German passengers.

Is Berlin that different from Paris? Do they have any sort of society in Berlin? Sabine thinks certain of the Germans looked stuffed with a boastful weariness. They talk of all the things they have in life. They shake their heads at a source of trouble. They don't want disorder. They want a life full of hope.

Now they sing again. Gustav is there in the midst of the group and he seems to be singing louder than the others. Gustav is such a healthy specimen. Sabine thinks of Leon's illness, Leon's promise that he'll die before they reach Cherbourg.

Ah yes, but a promise is only a promise.

Sabine watches them for no reason at all. She's bored. Every night is like every other night: Sabine and Leon sweating in the same bed, Sabine praying for the morning to arrive.

She feels an emptiness and gloom. What she wants is a liberation. She thinks of Paris, the suppers in smart restaurants. She wonders if her friends remember her. She tries to think of the name of that jeweler in Paris. Well, he's probably dead, isn't he? He was already quite old. She had her chance with that jeweler in Valparaiso. How stupid of her not to show him the emerald necklace, not to sell it to him. No, darling, you couldn't sell the necklace while you were in Valparaiso with Leon. Oh, damn Leon, he ought to have told her to sell it.

Sabine looks at the Germans again and she asks herself if they realize how silly they look. What silly people they are. Or is it the French who are silly? Why does Gustav feel so superior? Why does he feel so disdainful towards the South Americans? And Beatrix has such ugly collarbones. Sabine thinks of the whiteness of the blonde woman's skin. Beatrix has long blonde eyelashes. Sabine wonders if Beatrix was more beautiful as a girl. She imagines Beatrix as a girl in Berlin. Well, they don't lead the lives of unwashed peasants, do they? Then Sabine feels a spasm of sudden hatred for Beatrix. She has no understanding of it. She looks away. She wants to press her lips against something. Sabine quivers as she feels the trickling of sweat down the left side of her face.

*

They have the blanket on the floor, an old blanket that Sabine found in the closet next to the small desk that Jimenez uses to write his letters.

A stream of sunlight pours in through the open porthole.

Both Sabine and Eis are naked, Sabine's skin showing its cream-white color in the sunlight.

Eis is on his back on the blanket. His left knee is raised. Sabine sits on his chest, leaning backward, supporting her weight with her hands between his knees.

Sabine's nipples point upwards, two dark points lifted towards the ceiling.

Eis has his tongue extended, the tip of the tongue touching Sabine's sex.

Her sex is open and wet.

Sabine has her eyes fixed on Eis's face, her neck bent as she gazes down.

Eis holds her hips with his hands, his fingers clutching at her white flesh.

Now Sabine pushes forward a bit to get her sex more firmly against Eis's mouth, his nose touching her thicket, her open sex pushing against his lips.

Suddenly from the adjoining cabin comes the sound of music, a phonograph, the sounds of a piano.

Sabine continues looking down at Eis, watching his mouth, his lips. She can see the sweat on his forehead, his noble forehead, his pink face.

The climate has been awful in recent days, the ship steaming in the heat day and night, steaming through the canal from Balboa to Colon, steaming now in the open sea again.

Sabine continues to watch Eis's face.

How lovely it is to be without clothes like this. She wriggles her hips a bit. Yes, she can feel his tongue, his tongue in her sex.

Now she looks at the small writing desk again

and she sees a newspaper left by Jimenez on the chair. *La Nacion?* Sabine turns her head to look at the old newspaper from Santiago.

*

This morning Sabine is standing. She stands in the center of the cabin with her hands on Eis's head. Both of them are naked again, their skin white in the light from the porthole. Eis is on the floor with his body between Sabine's legs and his mouth on her sex. Sabine's left knee presses against Eis's right shoulder. She has her hands on his head, her fingers clutching at his hair.

Eis is sucking at her sex, his nose pressed into Sabine's pubic bush.

Sabine looks down at him, her neck bent as she looks.

Eis has his right arm curled around her left leg with his hand on her thigh. His fingers press into the white flesh of her thigh, pressing into the white skin.

Behind Sabine, the blue sky is visible through the porthole. It's almost noon, the air in the cabin stifling.

Is Sabine smiling? Her body trembles slightly.

Eis's neck is in an awkward position, his head motionless.

Sabine seems relaxed, her face calm, her pelvis thrust forward.

Now Sabine closes her eyes a moment.

The only sound is a distant throbbing of the ship's engines.

Sabine opens her eyes again and she turns her head to the side. A slight flush appears in her face, a pink glow suffusing over her cheeks.

She looks down at Eis again; she looks down at his mouth.

Eis continues to suck at Sabine's sex. He continues moving his tongue as she holds his head with her hands.

But his mouth has not moved; his neck is still bent back in an awkward position. His fingers are still clutching at her thighs.

Sabine slowly moves her hips, slowly pushing her sex against his upturned face.

*

And here is Sabine on the bed with her head on a pillow, still dressed, Sabine and Eis still dressed, both in white, Sabine on her back with her dress pulled up, her legs in white stockings, her left legs raised in the air, her white shoe pointing at the ceiling.

The fingers of Sabine's left hand can be seen extended over her mound, her fingertips just touching her sex.

Sabine's thighs are spread wide with her right leg flat on the bed and her left leg raised in the air.

The insides of her thighs are cream-white in color.

Her sex is open, the petals visible, her source exposed.

She has a dreamy look on her face, her mouth slightly open, her lips wet.

Eis is seated on the floor, leaning towards Sabine, his face close to her buttocks, his right cheek actually pressing against the lower part of her left buttock. His nose is flattened out as it presses against her left buttock. He has his tongue extended, the tip of his tongue tickling the dark little eye of her bottomhole.

Eis has sweat on his forehead.

Now Sabine quivers. Her left leg, the leg which is raised in the air, begins to tremble. She swings the leg a bit, her shoe still pointing at the ceiling but the leg now swinging slowly from side to side.

Eis has his flies unbuttoned, his penis and his testicles protruding from his open trousers, the knob of his organ pink and bloated.

Eis holds his swollen organ in his left hand as he continues licking Sabine.

Her leg moves again. The toe of her shoe still points at the ceiling, but her leg moves.

*

This is a grey day, the tropical rain splattering against the porthole, the interior of the cabin hot and damp and the corners in shadows.

Eis is naked on his knees, his rump in the air, the grey light gleaming on his white rump.

Eis seems to be in pain, his head back, his mouth hanging open.

Sabine stands behind Eis. She wears leather boots that cover her calves. Apart from the boots she's naked. Her skin glows, one side of her body catching the light from the porthole.

Sabine leans forward, her full breasts hanging with their weight.

She has her right foot planted on Eis's back, the toe of her boot on his spine, the heel just above the curve of his buttocks.

Around Eis's neck is a collar and attached to the collar is a metal chain that Sabine holds with her right hand.

Eis's mouth continues to hang open.

In Sabine's left hand is a short stick, the end of the stick touching Eis's left buttock.

His mouth still open, Eis continues to rest the weight of the front part of his body on his elbows.

Sabine's left hand moves and the stick strikes Eis's rump on the left side.

His mouth opens even further.

Sabine's right hand moves and the chain pulls at Eis's neck, pulling his head back as he continues opening his mouth.

Music suddenly starts in the adjacent cabin: Caruso singing an aria from Pagliacci.

Eis moves his mouth, but whatever sound Eis makes is drowned out by the voice of Caruso.

*

One morning on the deck, Eis talks to Sabine about Germany.

"It's a resurrection," he says. "It's our last hope."

"I don't understand."

"Hitler is our last hope. The last hope of the German people for survival. I have faith in Germany. I believe in honor and freedom. Hitler has brought the deliverance of millions. Don't you see, darling? It's a new life we have. The French will join us, you'll see. In any case you must understand that what we offer is strength and joy."

"The future of Europe," he says.

"Gustav, I don't understand."

"We had a difficult time after the war. Now we do a housecleaning. We clean up the Fatherland, throw out all the garbage and make a wonderful country again. I want you to see Berlin in the spring. Don't you think you could live in Berlin?"

Later in the cabin he smiles at her and he says he wants to suck her breasts.

"I want your nipple in my mouth."

His eyes are shining as he mumbles something about a new age.

Is it madness?

Sabine holds her breast to his mouth. She looks down at Eis sucking at her breast and she wonders about these Rhinelanders.

Dear God, what to they want? And is Berlin really so pleasant in the spring?

Chapter Eleven

*

His hair like the color of sand, Doctor Arthur Gordon stands there shading his eyes from the sun.

"He's not strong. I've examined him again and he's not strong."

The sea birds continue screaming. Sabine is half-reclined on a deck chair with her face protected by a large yellow hat.

"What?"

"Monsieur Mabeuf is not strong."

"Oh, do sit down."

Doctor Gordon lowers himself to sit in the chair beside her. He peers at Sabine, but the yellow hat hides most of her face and he finds it impossible to see her eyes.

"He needs a better heart," Arthur says.

"And, I need an apartment in Paris. Arthur, do you have any idea how awful it is to be in Paris and have nowhere to live?"

"I suppose you'll find something."

"And if I don't? I won't have any money, you know. What's a woman to do then except hang herself?"

Doctor Gordon looks away. He looks at strollers on the foredeck. He narrows his eyes against the glare of the sun as he looks at the strollers.

Sabine raises the yellow hat now and she glances at Arthur. He seems so unconcerned about her future. His face is so empty of anything, as empty as the blue sky.

I want clouds, Sabine thinks. I'm tired of the empty sky. I want clouds in the sky again.

"Arthur, don't you have any sympathy for me?"

"You know how much I adore you."

"I don't think you do. I think you pretend you do but you really don't. Are you certain you have no money in England? Don't you have a family?"

She touches his arm. Doctor Gordon stares at her fingers as they rub against his wrist.

But his face still has a blank look.

"I'm afraid I don't have anything."

"You don't like me. But you seem to like me enough when you're on your knees in front of me."

Doctor Gordon blushes, his cheeks, his forehead turning a bright pink in the sunlight.

"Don't be cruel, Sabine."

"I need a future."

A shadow falls over them. The Italian couple again. Lucia Forli holds the long white dress against her meager thighs.

Doctor Gordon talks about Leon again. He says Monsieur Mabeuf needs looking after, a valet or an attendant to see to his needs.

Sabine glances at the Italians and then she looks at the doctor again.

"He's stronger than you think."

"Who is?"

"My Leon, you fool. He's not that weak when he's at me in the cabin."

Doctor Gordon trembles. He shows his jealousy. Is he unhappy? His eyes are so blue as he gazes at Sabine.

Sabine is amused. She doesn't mind that Doctor Gordon is jealous. But even in his jealousy his face is as empty as ever.

The coast of Cuba is visible now. And the clouds have arrived. Sabine claps her hands as she sees the white clouds over Cuba.

Doctor Gordon talks about Cuba in a dull voice.

"Will you be going to the carnival?"

"Yes of course."

"With Monsieur Mabeuf?"

"And why not?"

"It might be too much for him."

"But he's already insisted he wants to go. Besides, if he's about to die anyway, I don't see what difference it makes."

"I'm afraid the excitement won't be good for him."

"When you first examined him, you said you couldn't find anything wrong."

"Yes, but one can't be certain."

Then Doctor Gordon touches her thigh. He begs to see her privately. He pleads.

"I must see you."

But Sabine makes a sound of irritation as she pushes him away.

"I'm too unhappy, darling. You do know how unhappy I am."

*

Unhappy enough to cry.

Sabine awakens unhappy in the morning and she cries again. She feels so alone. She wants to triumph over them, but she feels so alone now. She thinks of Gustav and his wife. She thinks of the meetings with Gustav, his liking for feverish conversations in the morning. What can I do without the aid of wealth? Sabine thinks. She remembers the railroad station when she arrived in Paris as an orphan. Her aunt and her uncle seemed so happy to see her, and how for one single moment she had the fantasy that her mother still lived in her aunt.

I am not obliged to Gustav. He thinks I refuse him because of some kind of vexation. He describes to Sabine the image of one hundred thousand stormtroopers saluting simultaneously at a rally for the Fuhrer.

Am I guilty of anything?

Sabine shudders and a moment later she begins to cry again.

*

"They're all mad," Leon says.

"Who is, darling?"

"The Germans. The Nazi bastards are all mad."

Leon has come out with her on the deck to sit in the shade awhile. He wanted it. After an hour of playing cards with him in the cabin, Sabine couldn't take it any more and she told him so. She told him she would faint if he didn't come out with her.

He wants to go on. He's talking now as if his impending death has been degraded from a probability to a possibility. He says he wants to begin again. But yet at times Sabine thinks that Leon looks so weak, so helpless, so much like a man nearing the end.

"In any case, the Germans bore me," Sabine says.

Leon laughs, a hot and bitter laugh that annoys Sabine.

You're like other women," Leon says. "You like the boots."

"Darling, let's not have an ugly scene. You know I don't like ugly scenes."

"He's always looking at you."

"Who is?"

"That bastard Eis."

Sabine refuses to reply. In her own way she understands Leon; she understands his doubts.

And I have my fears and sufferings.

*

Laughter now.

It's carnival in Havana.

Harlequins and buffoons everywhere, the streets and balconies filled with spectators, people jostling each other in the roads, old and young amusing themselves in costumes out of fashion for a century, women dressed as men and men dressed as women and all of them giggling under the rouge and powder and swirls of black lace.

And the masks. A jack of diamonds, a clown, a satyr, and here and there a face betrayed as the mask falls.

Leon is delighted. He stands with Sabine as they watch the women and children in the carriages toss flowers and candy at each other.

"Lord, what fun," Leon says.

Sabine enjoys the way the Cuban men look at her, these dark-eyed men with their white suits and long cigars.

She wears a white silk dress and white shoes and the emerald necklace Leon gave her when they left Paris.

Leon wants to see everything. He pulls at Sabine's hand. He points and laughs when he sees something amusing.

Then a girl rushes up to Leon and kisses him and Leon beams.

"It's marvelous!"

The girl's breasts vibrate under her blouse as she dances away.

Sabine teases Leon about the way he reacts to the Cuban women.

"You fancy them," Sabine says.

"But look how wonderful it is."

"Darling, it's a carnival."

His face is red, his forehead glistening as people jostle them back and forth.

Peals of laughter around them.

Sabine remembers Doctor Gordon's warning about Leon. She looks at his red face. No, he mustn't die yet. It's much too soon.

She takes his arm.

"Let's rest awhile."

"But I'm not tired," Leon says.

Sabine pulls at his arm.

"Darling, we do need to rest awhile."

He finally agrees to sit down at a table in a café. Now his exhaustion shows, his breathing heavy as he wipes his red face.

Two men at a nearby table are looking at Sabine. She notices their eyes, the dark eyes staring at her, undressing her, peeling the clothes off her back layer by layer. Now they have her down to nothing and she's completely naked to them. Yes, she likes it; she quivers. Does Leon notice it? She crosses her legs, always aware of the eyes of the Cubans, teasing them with her ankles and calves.

She feels happy.

A group of children run in front of the café shouting something about the clowns.

Yes, Sabine feels happy.

So many children.

Then Sabine suddenly feels how alone she is, how completely alone she is, like a rotting lily floating all by itself in a murky pond. No, not a pond, it's a river. It's a grey river that carries her along.

"I want to walk again," Leon says.

"Don't be stupid."

Will he cry? All this complexity. She doesn't want it. All she ever wanted was the peace of simplicity. Men think only of having their own fun.

I'm not a fool, Sabine thinks. I want to be an old lady of means. I want certain comforts in my declining years.

She wonders if Leon ever thinks of her financial difficulties, her prospects. She's his mistress, after all. The script for the comedy says the poor fool is supposed to look after her.

"Please, Sabine, let's walk again."

"Doctor Gordon says you're going to get well again."

What a lie it is. Sabine, what do you want?

Leon shakes his head.

"I'm going to die."

He's resigned to it. He does look on the edge of death. Now the children are shouting again, running back and forth in front of the café as they throw sugarcoated candies at each other.

The two Cuban men are staring at Sabine again. She's afraid to look at them. She looks at Leon's face instead, at the sweat on his forehead.

"Go back to the ship," Sabine says.

"What?"

"I said go back to the ship. You must do it, Leon."

"I refuse."

"Darling, I insist. The excitement is too much for you."

She orders it. She says she'll remain alone on shore. When Leon still refuses, she threatens to leave him immediately.

"If you refuse to look after your own health, then I won't be bothered with you."

He wipes his face.

"Yes, you're right. I don't feel well."

He takes fifty pesos out of his pocket and he hands the notes to Sabine.

She leaves the café table and she helps Leon into a taxi at the curb. He waves at her and she blows a kiss at him.

The children again. A small boy crashes into Sabine's leg and she gasps. The boy laughs at her, throws a candy at her and suddenly vanishes.

Shadows now.

A smell of roses and the noise of the street entering a room through the open shutters.

The two Cubans are naked, standing near the open window with Sabine between them.

She wears nothing but the emerald necklace.

One of the Cubans is kissing her. Maybe his name is Juan. Or maybe the other one is Juan and this one is Pedro. She has her face raised to accept the kiss, her mouth open to accept his tongue. His left hand is down at her belly, his fingers curled to penetrate her sex.

The other Cuban is behind her, leaning forward with his chin on her right shoulders, his right hand closed over her right breast. She touches him: she has her right hand behind her back and her fingers touching his organ and the bulge of his testicles.

The carnival is going on full blast in the street and the noise through the open window is defeating.

Juan keeps moving his tongue in Sabine's mouth. His fingers move in her sex, his thumb grazing her clitoris again and again.

Pedro pinches Sabine's nipple as she drops her hand a bit to curl her fingers under his heavy testicles.

Sabine's legs begin trembling.

Now the loud burst of a trumpet comes in from outside, first one trumpet and then two and then it sounds like a dozen trumpets blasting at each other.

Sabine keeps her mouth open as she groans

against the mouth that is kissing her.

*

This is the brown sofa not far from the open window and now a small lamp has been lit to make the Cubans and Sabine more visible.

Someone is shouting again outside the window.

Juan is seated on the sofa and Sabine is seated on his lap with her back to his face and her thighs wide apart and Juan's organ completely penetrating her sex.

Pedro is standing close to Sabine and Juan, Pedro's belly close to Sabine's head and his penis filling her wide open mouth.

Sabine's face is glistening with sweat now.

Pedro moves his hips slowly, his organ sliding slowly in and out of Sabine's mouth.

Juan squirms under Sabine and the base of his thick penis stretches the lips of Sabine's sex even further.

Sabine's breasts look swollen, her nipples thick, the white skin of her breasts glistening with sweat in the heat of the room.

The horns are blaring again outside, but this time the horns are not in synchrony, each trumpet blaring on its own, waiting, blaring again, the sounds of the various trumpets overlapping, the sounds of the horns almost continuous with each other.

Sabine moves both hands. She reaches down with her left hand to take hold of Juan's testicles. She reaches up with her right hand to do the same to Pedro.

Her mouth continues to be stuffed with Pedro's

organ.

Now Sabine's fingers move up from Juan's testicles to the base of his penis. She moves her fingers across the breadth of his penis, back and forth, back and forth.

Pedro continues to slide his organ in and out of Sabine's wide open mouth.

Sabine closes her eyes.

Her knees move towards each other, but then they move apart again.

She keeps her eyes closed as her mouth is filled.

*

The lamp is still lit and now Sabine is on her back on the sofa with her right leg raised and resting on Juan's left shoulder and Juan is kneeling between her open thighs with his organ pushing inside her sex while Pedro balances himself over Sabine's head to get his penis inside her mouth.

Sabine holds the penis in her mouth with her fingers.

Her right leg trembles as Juan slowly moves his organ in and out of her open sex.

*

Groaning now.

Sabine lies on her side with Juan's organ in her mouth and her right knee pulled all the way back to her right shoulder.

Pedro kneels at the lower end of Sabine's body, his belly pressed against her buttocks, his thick penis slowly pushing inside her stretched anus.

Juan clenches his teeth.

Pedro mumbles something in Spanish.

Sabine groans again as Pedro pushes forward.

*

When Sabine comes out of the Hotel Savilla, the streets are still crowded, the air is still filled with a smell of incense and violets, the clowns and buffoons are still waddling and waving their arms at everyone.

Sabine is feeling the rum now. The Cubans insisted she drink a little rum with them and now the rum has made her feet unsteady.

Sabine laughs at herself as she maneuvers through the crowds in the streets.

She thinks of Leon. Poor Leon. He needs a nurse. He needs someone to look after him.

The carnival is still in full swing, the streets bustling, the masks, the laughter, the singing making Sabine's head ache.

She makes her way through the streets at random, and then finally she finds a crowded café and she enters it.

Does she know anyone here? Inside the cafe Sabine is immediately called and when she turns she sees Gustav and Beatrix Eis at a table, Gustav with his arms raised as he calls to her.

"Please . . ."

*

Gustav and Beatrix are not alone.

Sabine is introduced to a Mr. Calvin Wacker, an American on his way from Panama to England.

"In the banana business," Mr. Wacker says. "I grow the best bananas in Panama."

Sabine has a sense of abandonment now. How amusing it is to find Gustav and his wife, Gustav with his glowing cheeks and his noble forehead and his eyes filled with such reverence for Sabine.

But Sabine ignores Gustav.

The four people chat about the carnival.

"And where is Monsieur Mabeuf?"

"On the ship, of course. He's not well."

"How awful. It must be the food."

"It's not the food, it's his heart."

"Ah yes, his heart," Beatrix says.

Gustav seems nervous. He laughs too much. He stares at Sabine as he talks and laughs. Sabine wonders how much Beatrix knows about her husband. The ice-blue eyes of Beatrix reveal nothing.

"I don't like Havana," Beatrix says. "The people are too rude."

Gustav laughs.

"My love, it's a fiesta."

"Too rude and too dirty. They don't wash. They seem to be interested in nothing but money. All these children with their hands out begging for coins."

"Not here in Havana."

"Then it was Ecuador."

"No, I think it was Peru."

"I don't like any of it."

Darkness is falling quickly outside. The restaurant has an air of gaiety, people calling to each other, the waiters rushing from one side of the room to the other.

Sabine is amused by the numerous prostitutes

in the café, the dark-eyed girls with red lips and soft arms. The men smoke cigars and count their bank notes as the girls lean against their shoulders.

"I'm hungry," Sabine says. "I think I'd like some dinner."

Beatrix looks bloodless.

"Yes, it's time."

Mr. Wacker rolls his eyes.

"Let's do the town."

Gustav laughs again.

"Yes, what a fine idea!"

Sabine agrees to join them in a tour of the nightclubs. A diversion. What a bore to be on the ship again with Leon. And Gustav is so amusing when he's nervous like this. He's completely unscrewed at the idea of having his wife and Sabine at the same table.

They have dinner in a noisy restaurant, and then after that they move to a nightclub in the entertainment quarter. Sabine thinks about Beatrix, her bony hands and her blue eyes. Gustav seems happy. Beatrix and Wacker seem to enjoy each other. Does Beatrix like bananas?

Gustav puts his hand on Sabine's knee, his fingers stroking the lower part of her thigh.

Beatrix and Wacker dance together and Beatrix looks content in the arms of the American.

Sabine decides Beatrix is a complete bore, nothing in the ice-blue eyes and nothing in the head.

"I adore you," Gustav says to Sabine.

"Not here, you fool."

The nightclub entertainment begins. First a

stupid act by two clowns. The American Wacker laughs at them. Then six girls trip out of somewhere to do a silly dance in a circle. They shake their breasts, roll their buttocks and toss their feathers around like a group of bedraggled chickens. Then finally the star attraction arrives: a beautiful Cuban girl who proceeds to remove her clothes to the beat of a drum.

The girl is soon naked, wearing only red shoes with pointed heels.

Beatrix seems annoyed.

Gustav laughs and makes a banal comment about the girl's buttocks.

The American Wacker is rolling his eyes again.

Sabine finds the girl interesting. The girl's mound is hairless, the top of the vertical mouth just visible as a deep slit, a dark little thing between two full lips, as dark as the nipples that look so saucy as they bounce to the drum.

When the girl retreats, the floor is cleared and the patrons dance again.

Sabine is bored once more. What an awful evening.

Beatrix insists on dancing with Wacker. She says it's too boring for a woman to dance with her own husband.

Gustav flushes.

Gustav is happy to dance with Sabine, but Sabine thinks dancing is such a sweaty business. She thinks Gustav is a fool. But the money, darling. Yes, the money. She thinks of her future again, her dismal prospects, the difficulties she will have in Paris.

Now Sabine refuses to dance any more. She

rebels against the tobacco smoke and sweat and the stink of stale rum hanging over the tables.

She walks away from Gustav and she sits down.

Gustav hurries to sit beside Sabine, his hand on her thighs again, his fingers sliding over her knees, fondling her knees as he pants beside her.

Sabine pushes his hand away.

"Don't be an idiot."

Gustav blushes, reverence in his eyes as he looks at Sabine.

"If only I could take you away with me."

"Well, why don't you?"

"I don't have anything. Everything belongs to Beatrix."

Sabine stares at him.

"What?"

"Yes, it's true."

"Tell me . . ."

And Sabine is told.

It's Beatrix who has the money.

Blue-eyes has everything and Gustav has nothing.

Chapter Twelve

*

In 1922 Kleiber has a successful gallery. Kleiber is fashionable. All the new important painters want to hang their work in Kleiber's gallery. The aristocracy comes to look at the new important painters. The journalists come to look at the aristocracy. The students come to look at the journalists. Kleiber stands to the side rubbing his hands and smiling at everyone.

One evening Sabine agrees to attend one of Kleiber's opening parties at the gallery. She hardly ever goes; she hates the crush, the snotty society talk, the way Kleiber ignores her these days. Oh yes, he ignores her now. After two years with him, it's obvious to Sabine that the affair is dying. Well, sooner or later it needs to happen, doesn't it? These things don't last forever. As she stands there in a corner, stands there away from the mob with a glass of champagne in her hand, Sabine tells herself that she really hates Kleiber. She hates Kleiber and she hates the painters. She hates the paintings too. The pictures all look crazy to her, the world upside down and inside out. What's it all coming to when you can't look at a painting without feeling the world's gone mad? But of course no one seems to care. Kleiber's gallery of three rooms in Rue Jacob is bursting apart as people continue to push their way inside.

Then a man approaches Sabine, a gentleman, tall, thin, grey hair at his temples, the women around them turning to have a look at him and Sabine.

Well, who is he?

He talks to Sabine about the champagne, about the paintings, about Kleiber. He says he's acquainted with Kleiber. He introduces himself as Monsieur Henri Daurez.

"And you're Sabine Boulanger."

"Yes, but how did you know that?"

"I noticed you and I asked Kleiber."

In a few moments Sabine is surprised to learn that Henri Daurez is a deputy cabinet minister. The Ministry of Industrial Development. Sabine quivers. She thinks of the Palace, the guards in Fauborg Saint-Honoré, the motorcyclists rushing from one district to the other, the smell, the taste of money and power.

He does have interesting hands. Sabine looks at the minister's hands and she quivers again. At twenty-two she's not such a child any more.

They talk. He's charming. They look at some of the paintings together. Sabine is happy. The minister's eyes are on Sabine's breasts. She thinks of his position. She thinks of the motorcycles again, the black leather helmets.

When Daurez offers to drive Sabine home in his car, she immediately agrees.

"I'll get my coat," Sabine says.

She navigates her way through the crowd to the back room where she left her coat with one of Kleiber's young flunkies.

"Maurice?"

"Yes, miss?"

"Who's that man? The one standing near that brown painting?"

Maurice squints at the other side of the crowded room.

"Henri Daurez. He's a minister of something."

Sabine leans towards the mirror on the wall as she puts more lip rouge on her lips.

"Are you sure?"

"Yes of course," Maurice says.

With Daurez in the back of his chauffeur-driven car, Sabine quivers again.

"Everyone seems to know you."

Daurez is amused

"Yes, I think so."

He puts his hand on her knee. He talks about his responsibilities, the future of France.

"Kleiber told me wonderful things about you," Daurez says.

"Did he?"

When Daurez brings her hand to the front of his trousers, Sabine turns to stone. The chauffeur? The driver is oblivious. Sabine relaxes. Yes, why not? She thinks of the motorcycles again. She runs her fingertips over Daurez's declaration of interest. She's flattered, of course; the deputy minister is armed and ready. The streets move by the car windows. Daurez helps Sabine get his organ exposed. He covers her hand with his as she closes her fingers around his rigid stalk.

"It will help relax me," Daurez says.

Sabine moves her hand up and down. Her fingers work at relaxing the Deputy Minister of Industrial Development. For the glory of France, the Palace, the motorcyclists. Daurez provides a white linen handkerchief. He covers his knob and groans as Sabine's fingers continue the process of relaxation to the end.

"That was perfect," Daurez says.

The white linen handkerchief returns to his pocket.

Sabine agrees to have dinner with Daurez the following evening.

The hell with Kleiber, Sabine thinks. The future is something exciting again.

*

Exciting, yes. The next evening Sabine is in a restaurant with Henri Daurez, a private room, sequestered, hidden from the mob outside, the waiters gliding in and out as they carry one course after the other.

Sabine and Daurez sit beside each other on a velvet bench and Daurez leans against her. He smiles at her.

"You make my heart warm," he says.

Sabine lifts her chin, an attempt to be suave.

"I don't know anything about you."

"My wife is a cold woman."

His eyebrows move up and down as he talks about his wife, his two daughter, the history of his family in Deux-Sevres.

Sabine dreams of the money, the power, the elegant manners.

After the restaurant, Daurez takes her to a flat that he rents near the Rue de Grenelle. The chauffeur is like a mummy, a dead man driving the car, his head never turning, not a sound out of

· 145 ·

his thin mouth.

The flat isn't much, nothing more than a bed-room and a small sitting room. Daurez lights a few candles, pours a little cognac and kisses Sabine's forehead. Another kiss, this time his wet lips on the nape of her neck and Sabine quivering as he begins to undress her.

He mumbles as her body is exposed. She continues sipping the cognac as his fingers work to peel her clothes away. He fondles her buttocks, first a gentle stroking and then a more forceful squeezing. He mumbles again as he leans forward to suck the points of her breasts. Sabine shudders as she feels his mouth on the flesh, his wet lips.

Then finally she's naked and he wants her on the sofa, her legs apart so that he can look at her sex.

"Like a goddess," he says.

His eyes are glowing. Sabine shudders at the fire in his eyes as he gazes at her bijou. Oh, those eyes. She likes to be looked at. She does like to be looked at.

Then he mumbles again and he sails in like a hawk to get his mouth on the target.

Sabine groans. She looks down and she can see nothing but his nose and forehead and the care-fully flattened hair on his head. Never mind, she thinks. It's not bad; it's not bad at all. She pulls back one knee. She rubs her knee with her fingers as Daurez continues his feeding.

It goes on and on, an endless sucking of her sex, his head nestled between her white thighs, his nose buried in the forest of dark hair that covers her mount. The Deputy Minister of Industrial

Development. Each time the phrase rings in Sabine's head, a great shudder passes through her body.

Then finally Daurez pulls away from her.

"Don't move," he says. "I want to look at you."

He wipes his mouth with a handkerchief. He proceeds to undress with his eyes always on Sabine. Methodical undressing. Everything in its proper order, each piece of clothing properly removed and folded and placed on a chair.

Daurez has a lean body and a lean organ, a lean spear shaking with impatience.

He mumbles something again and he lies down on the carpet.

Sabine stares.

"Your foot," Daurez says. "Do it with your foot."

Dear God.

Sabine unwinds herself to leave the sofa and move to Daurez.

She stands over him. Does he want the left foot or the right foot? The question in her head drives her crazy with uncertainty. She gives him the right. She presses her foot down on his hot flesh. She begins moving her foot without being told.

I must learn something about industrial development, Sabine thinks.

Daurez groans.

He groans again and Sabine watches the pale milk spurting out on his belly.

She still holds the glass of cognac in her left hand. Sabine looks at the cognac now and she moves her wrist to swirl the cognac in the light of the nearest candle.

*

"Diversion," Daurez says.

"What?"

"A man in my position needs a sensible diversion. You can see that, can't you? Ah, my sweet, what a beauty you are. Such grace."

He kisses her fingers and then he sits up and he shrugs his shoulders.

"What do you think?"

"What do I think about what?" Sabine says.

"I need your advice, darling. I have great need for relaxation these days and I'm wondering if you might help me."

He sits down in one of the chairs near the mantel. He's wearing a robe now, a long blue robe that makes him look like a monk. But of course he's not a monk, he's the Minister of Industrial Development.

Daurez continues to talk about his need for diversion, for relaxation, for an hour or two of freedom each day. Can Sabine help him? He says where they are now is most convenient for him, no more than a short walk from the ministry.

"Is it too soon, darling? Am I putting my case too soon?

Now he seems in the midst of confusion. He leaves the chair and he comes to Sabine to kiss her. He stands before her and he leans down to kiss her forehead. His robe has opened and Sabine finds herself staring at his dangling penis. His organ is quite thin when it's limp like this. She thinks of the other lovers she's had. Well, this is the Minister of Industrial Development, isn't it? She remembers the feel of his penis spurting under her bare foot. She remembers how pleasant it was. She likes it. She has her whims. She finds it exciting to watch Daurez groaning beneath her foot.

"We might discuss it," Daurez says. We might discuss the conditions of our proposed relationship.

But not yet. He wants to frolic with her again. He leads her to the bedroom and he hints that he wants her mouth.

"Darling, it's impossible to resist your lips."

The Minister of Industrial Development is naked on the bed. He smiles at Sabine as he beckons to her.

"I'm sure you have a divine talent for it. You do, don't you, darling?"

Sabine quivers as she gazes at his handsome organ. Now that it's awake again, the tool of the minister is more formidable. Almost beautiful. Sabine decides that Daurez has an organ that's almost beautiful. A penis to be sucked. White and smooth and with a lovely pink crown that makes her mouth water. Oh Sabine. She never responds like this with Kleiber. She leans over Daurez and she runs her tongue over his pink knob. She feels his trembling flesh with her lips.

Daurez groans.

"You're magnificent."

Sabine plants a series of darting kisses up and down the length of his organ. She sucks at the tiny hole in the tip of his knob. She has the taste of Daurez on her tongue. Once again she thinks of the palace and the motorcyclists and the photographs of the various ministers that appear so frequently in the newspapers. And here is the Minister of Industrial Development and she has his penis in her mouth. She opens her mouth wider and she captures him; she captures Daurez; she fills her mouth with the bloated knob of his organ.

Daurez groans as he feels her lips. Sabine senses his passion rising. Yes, she wants it. She keeps his organ in her mouth. She begins a slow sucking, a slow movement of her lips, a slow bobbing of her head.

Daurez groans again. He trembles in his enjoyment. Sabine turns her head to watch his face. She sucks his penis with more insistence. More movement now. She bobs her head more rapidly until his crisis approaches. She holds her lips over the knob of his penis as he spends.

Well, it's not the same, Sabine thinks. It's the sperm of the Minister of Industrial Development and it's not the same.

*

A bright morning in Rue de Grenelle.

Three months have passed and now Sabine opens her eyes in the bedroom. She's had the room redone, new paper on the walls, a lovely pink silk, new furniture, the large gilt mirror she found in Clichy. When Daurez is in a good mood he can be quite generous.

Sabine stretches on her bed, a lazy stretching of her limbs under the warm sheet. She yawns as her hand reaches out to the bell cord.

In a few moments the maid enters, the cheery-faced girl Sabine brought with her from Kleiber's flat.

"Good morning, miss."

"What day is it?"

"It's Thursday, miss."

The maid brings Sabine her breakfast on a tray. Sabine sips the hot chocolate as she tries to remember her plans for the day.

"Are you sure it's Thursday?"

"Yes, miss. Monsieur Daurez said he expects to be here before noon. It's almost ten, you know."

The maid bustles about the room as Sabine watches her. Finally Sabine yawns again and she slips out of the bed. Daurez before noon. She doesn't much like Daurez before noon.

Sabine begins to get ready for the Deputy Minister of Industrial Development.

A bath. Her body powdered and perfumed. The maid sent out for flowers.

When Daurez arrives, his energy flows into the rooms in a great wave.

Daurez in the morning is an officer on the bridge of the Ship of France. Pink cheeks and a white smile and his eyes dancing with secret amusements.

He talks about his morning at the ministry. The constant signing of important papers. He quickly strips his clothes off and he stands there in the bedroom with his fingers running up and down his lean organ.

"I think about you even as I sign my papers."

Sabine still knows nothing about industrial development.

On the bed, Sabine tickles Daurez's penis and testicles with a feather while he kisses her bottom.

Kissing and licking.

Sabine enjoys Daurez's tongue. She quivers as she moves the feather over his testicles, around and around the two sources of her comforts.

Daurez hardly ever gets himself inside her. She submits when he wants it but she always hates it. She would rather have his tongue.

But today is one of the rare days and his energy is extreme. He fondles her buttocks. He licks up and down in the crack, licking and mumbling, his breath hot against her powdered flesh.

Sabine finally rolls over on her belly to have her bottomhole greased with pomade.

"I adore you," Daurez says. "Buy some new clothes if you like. There's a shop in the Vendôme with a very discreet manager. If you give him my name, you can choose anything you want. Would you like that, darling? A little present for my sweet dove? And this is my little present, isn't it? Lord, how exquisite you are. Such a perfect little rose. My Sabine has the most perfect little rose in all of Paris."

She lies flat on the bed, her cheek resting on her forearms as she listens to his constant prattling.

The chatter stops only during the few moments it takes Daurez to push his lean organ inside her back channel.

Sabine is annoyed. She tightens her sphincter around Daurez's penis. The chatter stops and now Daurez begins grunting.

Now Sabine is happy. The Deputy Minister of Industrial Development grunts like a pig when he uses the little one.

When the business is finished, Daurez is soon chattering again, in a hurry as he dresses, in a hurry as he brushes his coat.

Sabine remains on the bed as Daurez hurries back to his office to continue the industrial development of the French people.

*

A rainy evening, the rain splashing against the windows in Rue de Grenelle, the flat damp and Daurez's tobacco smoke filling the small sitting room.

Daurez looks unhappy. He's not talking with his customary verve. He sits with Sabine on the red sofa in the dim lamplight. A domestic scene; Sabine is amused at her own domesticity.

Sabine waits.

Before long Daurez begins talking about his wife. The cold one, he calls her. Madame Daurez is so cold and dull. Cold and dried out. Daurez mumbles as he searches for the right words. Sabine is annoyed.

"What?"

"She's getting ideas," Daurez says.

"Ideas about what?"

"She's becoming suspicious."

Sabine decides he's ridiculous. His eyes are so mournful.

"Maybe you're imagining it."

"She's a terror."

He mumbles again. Sabine has seen the wife—

that day in the Tuileries when Daurez passed with his wife on his arm. A sour-looking woman from Bordeaux, a woman with her nose in the air as she walks over the gravel in the park.

Another splash of rain on the windows as Sabine fidgets on the sofa.

*

A hurried morning again. Daurez sits in the Empire chair near the small fireplace. He wears a dark suit and he's hardly calmed down after the rush to Rue de Grenelle from his office. He leans forward, bending his head forward, bending his head forward, his back bent, his head forward and down as he fills his hands with Sabine's rump.

Sabine's derriére.

Daurez is kissing Sabine's derriére.

Sabine is naked, her back to Daurez, bending forward enough so that her hands touch her thighs just above her knees.

Not completely naked. She wears a black brassiere and shoes, the brassiere with its front cut away to show her breasts and nipples, an amusement brought by Daurez in a fancy box with a red silk ribbon. The shoes are slippers with high heels and black little pompons on the toes.

Sabine quivers as Daurez continues kissing her bottom. She turns her head, twists her head to the right in an attempt to look down at him over her right shoulder, but she can't manage it.

She makes due with the sounds of his kissing.

Her mouth is open.

Then the sounds are stopped as Daurez pulls

his face back. He fondles her bottom, his fingers digging into her flesh as he mumbles.

Sabine wriggles.

"What?"

He pats her bottom.

"It's finished. My wife knows everything."

Sabine rolls her eyes.

"But what can she do?"

"She's threatening a scandal."

Sabine tries to reason with him. Every man in Paris has a mistress. Why is Madame Daurez so different? And why is Henri so afraid of his wife?

Sabine learns: Daurez's position in society derives from his wife, the wealth and power of his wife's family.

"That's it," Daurez says.

He pulls away from Sabine, his hands pulling away from Sabine's buttocks, his saliva still drying on her white skin.

Chapter Thirteen

*

East of the Bahamas.

Sabine stands with Gustav at the stern of the Reina del Pacifico. Gustav keeps his hands on the rail as he gazes down at the boiling wake of the ship.

"We need to find a way to get rid of her."

The air is so clean this morning, not a hint of the smell of engine oil or rotting fish.

Sabine stares at Gustav.

"What do you mean?"

Gustav shrugs. His face is a bright pink in the sunlight.

"Get rid of her."

"But you're not serious."

"Yes, of course."

The breeze disturbs his hair, a strand or two falling across his noble forehead.

Suddenly a noise on the deck below them and a pair of hairy arms can be seen. A sailor heaves a pailful of garbage out of the stern of the ship.

Gustav is annoyed.

"What the hell!"

The garbage drops into the boiling wake, vanishes into the foam and then reappears again where the water is calm.

"Disgusting," Gustav says.

He pulls his hands away from the rail as if the rail has suddenly grown hot.

Sabine watches the garbage floating in the distance. Is that an empty candy box? Or is it merely the rind of a large melon?

"They ought to find some other way," Gustav says.

"I suppose the fish like it."

"Well, damn the fish.

He grips the rail again. He stands as stiff as a general at the rail as he talks about his wife. About Beatrix. The former Beatrix von Hauptmann.

Now the sea birds have arrived. The sea birds are calling. Sabine watches the sea birds as they attack the floating garbage.

Then Sabine turns and she sees the Italians again, the man and the woman walking arm in arm around the stern. The woman wears the same long dress, the same cloche hat, her thin neck bent a bit and her eyes in shadow.

"Does she have a lover?"

Gustav looks at Sabine.

"Who?"

"Your wife, Gustav. Does Beatrix have a lover?"

"It's impossible."

"Nothing is impossible."

"I would know it if she had a lover."

But Gustav's uncertainty is apparent now. He's afraid of his wife, the cold glance, the awful silence that comes when she's displeased.

Then on the deck below them the arms appear once more, the pail swinging, the garbage flying out of the stern of the ship and into the wake.

"Dear God," Gustav says.

They walk to the bow of the ship. Sabine thinks of Leon as they pass the entrance to the state-rooms. Eis continues talking about murdering his wife.

"It can be done," Gustav says.

Sabine is grateful to be free of the Italians, that frightful woman and the mummy whose arm she holds.

At the bow Gustav breathes in a great lungful of sea air.

"This is good."

"Is it?"

"Physical fitness is important. You don't know what we're doing in Germany. The world will see."

"I don't want to know about Germany."

"After Beatrix is gone everything will be wonderful with us. We'll have a large house, won't we? Near the Tiergarten. You'll see how lovely it is."

He's like a boy now, his eyes flashing as he talks about Berlin, his chin thrusting forward in his eagerness.

"The fact is I don't believe everything they say."

Sabine frowns.

"I don't know what you're talking about."

"All that Aryan crap. It's possible to be a good German without all that Aryan crap. The party doesn't need it. We'll just give the Jews to anyone who wants them."

"Gustav, I'm not German."

"When Beatrix is gone, everything will be good for us."

"Your idea is stupid."

"What?"

"I said your idea is stupid. This notion you have that you can murder your wife."

Gustav flushes.

"But it can be done."

"You're an idiot. I won't have anything to do with it."

The wind blows his hair again, a strand of hair curving down over his pink forehead.

*

Sabine rejects the idea of marriage. She thinks of her father, her girlhood, all those dreary days in the damp house in Vouziers. In any case, Gustav's passion is ridiculous. Will he be so generous as a husband? Will he be so reverent when his hands are shaking? Sabine remembers the look of utter boredom in her mother's eyes. Now she knows. She would not tolerate the status of a daughter-in-law. Then Sabine accuses herself of being silly. It's all an attempt to persuade herself not to marry Gustav. But in any case she can't marry him until Beatrix is gone, until Beatrix has passed away from the scene. You have no future that's promising, Sabine thinks. Your future is to struggle in despair. What she has is a future without hope. Some women are favored by a future with hope and some women are not. As a married woman she would have Gustav like a huge stone around her neck, a stone pulling her head down and bending her back like so many of these old women one sees in the markets.

And it doesn't last forever, Sabine thinks. The

attraction of that place between her legs will fade. Men will not come to her with their confessions. Gustav will find an adorable blonde to amuse him. He will not come to Sabine for his pleasures. Once the beauty is gone the woman is left with nothing but her bent back. The pigs move off to sniff at other treasures. How silly it is the way they hunger for it. It's all the same no matter what the class. One sees it in the social columns of the newspapers: the men sniffing at the women and the women giggling with joy in response. They want that hot flower between a pair of soft thighs. Even the priests roll their eyes whenever they think of it.

The world is no larger than my clitoris, Sabine thinks. She finds her pleasure in Gustav kneeling at the altar. Well, let them kneel; they all want it. Even that boy in Santiago. She held his head with her hands while he sucked at her fountain.

Darling, you're trembling.

And you must understand that Gustav is German. They're up to something, aren't they? Leon says it's going to be very bad. He says the Huns will be running throughout all Europe. We'll have our wretched warfare again.

Sabine tries to imagine Gustav as a warrior. What precisely is the personality of Gustav Eis? He's more romantic than Leon. Is he illegitimate?

I must learn about the Nazis. No, I don't want to know about the Nazis. I'll meet Gustav's mother and when I know her I'll decide. I'll sit with Gustav's mother in the evening and we'll drink tea and we'll discuss the flowers in her garden.

Darling, there's no need to love him. It's not to love or not to love. You've suffered too much, haven't you? You mustn't betray yourself on that account. Sabine, do you understand? The trouble with God is that He keeps His silences.

And Berlin? Is it possible to live with Gustav in Berlin? Darling, you must understand what is about to happen. Sabine considers the obscurities. A large black cloud darkens her mind. She sees herself at the entrance of a monstrous mausoleum, one of those huge German buildings one sees in the magazines. What sort of house will they have in Berlin? And the Nazis? Will Gustav march in those stupid parades?

Sabine remembers the sham Louis XV table in the house of her aunt and uncle. Does she want such a table in a house in Berlin? Gustav will have a house with a fence around it, a long black fence with a row of sharp points on the top to keep the Nazis out.

If I'm to be his mistress, I must learn something about the German temperament. Does he like children? Sometimes Gustav is such a child. He plays with his passions the way a child plays with his toys.

Sabine shudders now. She feels a sense of something. She feels a sense of impending doom.

*

One afternoon it rains. Leon sleeps in the cabin and Sabine walks to the salon to get free of him. The ship is now twenty-five days out of Valparaiso and everyone aboard seems hypnotized with boredom.

The wind slams the door open as Sabine enters the salon.

The room is almost empty, no more than a dozen passengers sitting quietly with their books and newspapers.

Alone in a corner, Beatrix Eis is turning the pages of a magazine.

Sabine approaches Beatrix. The blonde woman raises her head, looks at Sabine and offers a thin smile.

"How are you, Sabine?"

"Do you mind if I sit here with you?"

Sabine sits down and they begin chatting. Beatrix seems relaxed. The ice-blue eyes look at Sabine. Beatrix smiles as she holds the magazine in her hands.

Sabine is hopeful. Gustav is so stupid to think of murdering his wife. One must try to be clever first. Beatrix has such a firm jaw, such determined hands.

"Tell me about Berlin," Sabine says.

"Berlin?"

"I don't know anything about Germany."

Beatrix smiles.

"My life in Berlin is very quiet."

"This ship is a bore, isn't it? The food is so horrible."

"And how is your Leon?"

"He says he's dying."

"Yes, I know. I'm so sorry."

"The doctor says he can't be helped. Anyway, I think Leon is resigned to it."

"I tell Gustav to visit Leon, but Gustav is like a child sometimes. One day he's frightened and the next day his enthusiasm is ridiculous."

Not so much ice in the eyes now. Beatrix has lost her coolness to Sabine. The ice is melting. The Valkyrie sings a lullaby. Sabine quivers as the friendship begins. Beatrix laughs; her thin red lips keep moving as she laughs.

"I like you," Sabine says. "I like blondes."

Beatrix blushes, a flicker in the blue eyes, the hands moving constantly in her lap.

Beatrix fidgets. She seems uncertain. Sabine is amused.

It's done, Sabine thinks. Well, it's obvious, isn't it?

Sabine reaches out to touch the hand of Beatrix. For the first time Sabine notices that Beatrix has perfect fingernails.

*

The interior of the Eis cabin is like all the others; yellow stains on the walls, the furniture bolted, the porthole glass dull with grime.

Beatrix has her dress raised. Sabine stands close to Beatrix, but Sabine is still covered. Beatrix has her dress raised to the level of her waist and Sabine has her left hand on the blonde's right thigh. Sabine's palm covers the garter strap that holds up the grey silk stocking.

The short girdle that Beatrix wears is cut high enough in front to show her blonde nest.

Their heads touch as they look at each other.

Sabine moves her hand upwards and now her thumb is just grazing the curled blonde hair at the joining of the blonde's thighs.

Sabine's hand moves up and down over the

white skin above the stocking.

Beatrix trembles.

Their heads touch again as Sabine's hand continues the stroking.

*

On the bed now.

Both women are naked.

Sabine lies back on the bed with her head on the pillow and Beatrix lies between Sabine's legs, leaning back on Sabine with her head on Sabine's left shoulder.

The blonde has her head turned to look at Sabine's face.

Sabine has her arms around Beatrix, her left hand covering the small mount of the blonde's left breast, her right hand reaching down to the tuft of blonde curls below the blonde's belly.

Beatrix keeps her thighs well apart to expose her sex. She smiles at Sabine. They kiss. Sabine's mouth presses against the blonde's lips. Sabine pinches the blonde's left nipple.

Beatrix groans.

Sabine reaches further with her right hand, the arm stretched, the fingers searching for the blonde sex.

Beatrix widens the spread of her thighs.

Sabine looks down at the body in her arms. Such white skin. The blonde has such white skin.

*

Beatrix talks to Sabine about her life. She says that her home in Berlin is quite comfortable. She says she enjoys playing the role of a respectable woman.

"It's necessary to be of some importance, isn't it? I keep my days busy. I like to dress myself. I dress myself for myself and not for Gustav."

She knows that Gustav has other women. She doesn't care. She likes her jewels. She feels she has an obligation to her family. And of course to the Fatherland. One is obligated to live well and live according to the dictates of obligations. Her family has always known luxury and she can't imagine a life without it.

"My flowers," Beatrix says. "I have such lovely flowers in the garden. I adore Parma violets."

She adores the music of the truly German composers. She adores the new songs that one hears in the cabarets in Berlin.

"I have my own amusements, you see. It's not possible to live without one's own amusements."

*

And now Sabine is sitting up on the bed with her legs wide apart and Beatrix is leaning over her from the side. The blonde has her head down, the right side of her face touching the dark bush on Sabine's mound. Beatrix has her mouth open, her tongue extended as she slowly licks Sabine's clitoris.

Sabine gazes down, but she can't see more than the back of the blonde's head.

Sabine touches the blonde head, her fingers stroking the blonde hair.

Beatrix trembles as she keeps her tongue moving over Sabine's clitoris.

Sabine continues gazing at the back of the blonde head, the partly hidden face that rests on her belly.

*

"The eggs aren't cooked," Gustav says. "The fools ought to cook the eggs before they bring them to the table. I won't have it. I won't have my eggs uncooked."

Sabine ignores him as she sips her coffee. She looks away as the eggs are returned to the waiter.

"You'll have a divorce," Sabine says.

"What?"

"Beatrix will give you a divorce."

Gustav stops buttering his toast.

"Dear God."

"Isn't that what you want?"

His face becomes pale as he considers the loss of his wife's money.

"She won't give my anything."

"You're a stupid fool."

A flush comes to his face.

"I tell you she won't give me anything."

"You'll get whatever you want."

Sabine thinks of him on his knees, naked on his knees and crawling on the floor in Fernando's cabin.

Eis continues buttering his toast. Now his hands are trembling. The flush continues in his face as he slowly spreads the butter over his toast.

Chapter Fourteen

*

The cabin in the afternoon heat is like a steam-bath. Leon is sitting in a chair with his head leaning against the wall. Sabine is standing nearby. She has just lit a cigarette, and now she holds it in her right hand, her left hand supporting her right elbow as she puffs on the cigarette and blows the smoke into the air.

Leon looks miserable, his eyes mournful. Someone laughs in the corridor outside the door. The laughter continues for a few moments, and then it dies away gradually until there is silence again.

"I'll kill myself," Leon says.

Sabine turns away from him. The heat has caused her to perspire and her blouse is ruined. She looks at herself in the small mirror on the wall and she frowns.

"You're an idiot."

"I won't listen to you. You're a traitor to France."

Sabine ignores him. She stands in front of the mirror and she begins putting lipstick on her lips. She stops a moment to wipe the sweat off her forehead with a handkerchief. Then she carefully puts the handkerchief in the pocket of her skirt and she continues painting her lips.

"I'm still fond of you," Sabine says.

"I don't want to live any more."

Sabine finishes painting her lips, and now she looks down at her shoes. She wears white shoes, each shoe with a single strap across the instep.

"Leon, be sensible. I'll have nothing when you die. How can I possibly manage things when I'll have nothing?"

"Having you go to that pig Eis is too much."

Sabine looks at the bed, at the mess they've left, the sweat-soaked sheets pulled away and rolled up in a corner.

"You need to accept it."

"I can't."

"But why not?" Sabine says.

She turns to the mirror again. She discovers she doesn't like the way her lips are painted and now she removes the lipstick from her purse and she begins changing the shape of her mouth.

"He's a Nazi," Leon says. "You don't know anything about them."

He mumbles. He leans his head against the wall again. His lips continue working but nothing but mumbling comes out of his mouth.

"And what about Beatrix?" Sabine says.

Leon straightens up, his face flushed in the heat and his eyes wild.

"She's a Nazi too."

"Do you want her?"

Leon is astonished at the question. His eyes round, he watches Sabine as she pats her hair in front of the mirror.

"What do you mean?"

"I mean do you want her? Would you like to have her? I think you know what I mean."

Leon smiles. He makes a sound of amusement

in his throat.

"You can have her," Sabine says. "If you want her, you can have her."

Sabine looks at the mirror again and Leon stops chuckling.

"How do you know?"

"Darling, you need to trust me."

For a long moment Leon says nothing; and then he looks at Sabine and he nods.

"All right."

Sabine turns to him.

"Are you still going to kill yourself? Have you finished with that idiotic idea? I'll get Beatrix for you."

"I won't kill myself yet."

Now there is laughing outside the cabin again. Leon leans his head against the wall as before and he sighs.

Sabine looks at Leon, satisfied now that his equilibrium is restored.

"Leon, it's much too hot in here."

*

Beatrix is madly in love with Sabine. The adoration in the blonde's eyes is always there, always obvious. They meet each afternoon, sometimes in the salon, sometimes on deck. They whisper to each other, the whispers of feminine secrecies.

When they go to the Eis cabin, Beatrix reads poetry to Sabine. Goethe and Schiller. Beatrix says she no longer permits herself to read Heine. Sabine has no idea what the blonde is talking about. The names mean nothing to Sabine. The

Eis cabin is always so hot. They hold hands. Beatrix likes to show her blonde body. She likes to talk about her childhood in Saxony. Talking, talking. She confides a secret: she thinks the French are as Aryan as the Germans.

"But of course some of the French were contaminated by the Italians."

"What?"

"Darling, you're not listening," Beatrix says.

Sabine gazes at the blonde's throat, her pink nipples.

They pass langorous afternoons together on the bed, slow caressing, their fingers tapping and stroking, their palms wet with perspiration.

In the afternoon Gustav is forbidden to enter the cabin. Instructions from Beatrix. "He's like a mouse," Beatrix says. She wants total seclusion with Sabine. She wants hours of lovemaking. Each orgasm is a cataclysm, a long shuddering that goes on and on.

Beatrix likes to be naked in the cabin, her pink body glowing in the heat, her arms and legs entwined around Sabine as they roll on the bed. The blonde's eyes are happy as she opens Sabine's thighs, as she kneels to the ritual. Sabine lies back with her knees up and her face turned to the porthole to catch a glimpse of the blue sky. She looks at the sky as Beatrix sucks the liquid out of her sex, as Beatrix sucks her clitoris. On occasion Beatrix has her victory and Sabine shudders.

"I can feel it between my lips," Beatrix says.

She tells Sabine about her previous affairs with women. Her secrets. Gustav never knows. The shopgirls in Berlin are so easy. But one has to be very secretive now because of the revolution.

"Revolution?"

Beatrix laughs.

"Things are different in Germany now."

Sometimes they drink champagne in the cabin. Beatrix brings out her jewels to show them to Sabine.

"You have beautiful jewels too."

"But I don't have anything," Sabine says.

"You have that lovely emerald necklace. Was it a present from a lover?"

"Yes."

"I hate my marriage. I hate Gustav. He's a fool. He has no strength. He struts but he has no strength. I like a man to be strong."

Sabine wonders how rich Beatrix is, how rich the family. Is it mines again? She watches as Beatrix fondles her own breasts, the slender fingers dancing over the pink nipples.

"I love my breasts," Beatrix says. "I like to play with them. I like to watch the nipples get hard."

Then Beatrix is on her knees and she wants to suck Sabine again. Sabine sighs. She doesn't mind it. She opens her legs and once again she turns her face to the porthole to look at the sky.

*

It always possible to learn something new. Sabine remembers a girl in Santiago. One must be able to learn. In Santiago the streetcars were comfortable and efficient. Sabine remembers the girl with her charms exposed. Was her name

· 171 ·

Tomasina? Sabine remembers the girl lying naked on the narrow bed in that cluttered room. The pimp, the man who looked like a fool but who wasn't a fool, the pimp leered at Sabine before he finally closed the door to leave only the smell of his cigar in the room.

Sabine, you're a woman obsessed with erotic follies.

Yes, why not? The times with that girl was certainly the loveliest time she had in Santiago. The girl groaned as Sabine took her, Tomasina squirming her sex on Sabine's fingers. They sucked at each other's mouths. Tomasina sucked at Sabine's nipples. Sabine tickled her. Sabine fondled the girl's breasts and buttocks, her fingers in both holes, her mouth sucking at the girl's clitoris until the girl screamed.

Sabine, these games are madness.

One thrives on the indecency. She wanted that girl kneeling and she had that girl kneeling. At the end Tomasina whimpered as she begged Sabine not to leave her.

A quaint memory, darling. Sabine wonders if the girl ever thinks of her. Or maybe it's the pimp who thinks of her and not the girl. When Sabine first met the pimp, it was him she wanted. She wanted him thrusting at her while he was still dressed, his cigar in his mouth and his trousers at his ankles and his thick organ pounding in her sex as she bent over a crate somewhere. What madness to be taken by a pimp in such a position. No hardships, darling. When he offered the girl, you accepted. But darling you do enjoy men like that. She likes to see the sweat on their shoulders. She likes the smell of them. All those graceful boys she had in Santiago, the sweating boys who made love to her, the smell of sex in the stuffy rooms.

Am I a patroness? What she likes is the hard thrusting, the pounding of the penis in her dark cave. She often wonders what they think of her. What impression does she make? What do they think of this woman who likes to be taken like an animal? Is she an enlightened woman? Sabine remembers the way they look at her afterward. She remembers the intimacy of it. That boy who had her bent double near a window in the sunlight and then afterward the wonder in his eyes as he watched the sperm running out of her sex in a slow dribbling.

She feels it now. Sabine feels the wetness now along the insides of her thighs.

*

In the evening the sun is an orange ball sinking towards the far horizon. Sabine has just come out on the deck and now Doctor Gordon appears and he walks over to stand beside her at the rail.

"I know what you're doing," Doctor Gordon says.

Sabine turns to look at him, to look at his hair the color of sand.

"What do you mean?"

"You're carrying on with that German woman. It's nasty, isn't it?"

A breeze blows at Sabine's dress. She looks away. She looks down at her shoes.

"You're an idiot."

She walks away from him. Doctor Gordon

hurries after her.

"It's unnatural. I don't know why you want that sort of thing. It's awful, isn't it?"

Sabine stops and she faces him with anger.

"You fool!"

"Sabine, I beg you . . ."

"Are you bothered because she's German? You're the same, aren't you? The English and the Germans?"

"That's absurd. I don't care about that. I don't care about their little Fuhrer."

Sabine walks again and Doctor Gordon follows her. People are on the deck now, strolling casually in the cooling twilight.

"I want to be alone with you," Doctor Gordon says.

"You're a stupid little boy."

"His voice is urgent.

"Please, Sabine . . ."

"Maybe tomorrow."

In the west the sky is orange, a burning orange on the far horizon.

*

Sabine has brought Beatrix to Leon's cabin. The heat wave continues and in the early afternoon the cabin is unbearably hot. Beatrix and Leon are naked on the bed. Sabine sits in a chair near the open porthole, fanning herself with an old newspaper as she watches them.

The bodies on the bed are sweating and pink.

Leon is on his back, his eyes closed and his mouth open.

Beatrix leans over his belly as she sucks his

organ. Her lips are stretched by the hardness of his penis. Her face is sweating, and as she moves her head up and down the droplets of perspiration fall off her forehead and chin to drop to his belly and thighs.

Leon groans.

Sabine listens to the groan and she quivers. Is it the noise of a dying man?

Now Beatrix raises her head a moment to look at Sabine. The blonde's lips are wet. She looks at Sabine with unhappy eyes.

Sabine says nothing. The two women stare at each other a long moment, and then finally Beatrix returns to sucking Leon's penis.

In a moment the sounds of sucking can be heard again.

Leon continues to groan, his eyes closed, his mouth hanging open.

Then Beatrix pulls her face away again. She holds his organ with both hands, her eyes staring at it, at the dark red color of it. She seems hypnotized by the stiff penis. She moves her body forward now, climbing over Leon and mounting him. She takes his organ inside her sex, her pink nipples bouncing as she settles down on his belly.

Sabine continues to fan herself with the old newspaper.

Beatrix begins moving on Leon's organ, slowing up and down, Leon groaning as she moves.

Now Sabine leaves her chair and she walks across the short distance to the bed. She sits on the bed beside Leon and Beatrix. Sabine still holds the old newspaper in her hand and she begins fanning herself with it again.

Beatrix continues moving.

Then the blonde turns her head to kiss Sabine as she moves up and down on Leon's organ. The lips of the women touch. The blonde's lips are wet. Her hair has become unpinned and now she brushes it out of her eyes.

Beatrix returns her attention to Leon.

Still holding the old newspaper in her right hand, Sabine slowly runs her left hand over the blonde's back. Sabine's fingers slowly move down the spine to the curve of the buttocks.

The flesh of Beatrix is pink and firm to the touch.

Sabine holds the blonde's bottom as it continues to move up and down.

Now Beatrix turns her head and she kisses Sabine again with her wet lips.

Sabine moves her fingers. She touches the joining of penis and sex, the stretching of the pink mouth, the tight little hole between the blonde's buttocks.

Now it's Beatrix that groans, her chin raised and her mouth open as she continues moving her body.

*

"I do mean it, darling."

Beatrix has offered to give Gustav to Sabine. The blonde's eyes are amused. She looks at Sabine and then she looks down and she touches one of her nipples.

"Is it so very strange?"

"No," Sabine says.

"I'll give him something. I'm to inherit a

fortune and I suppose Gustav ought to have something. I don't want him, you know. He's nothing but a convenience for me. You do understand, don't you?"

"Yes."

"Darling, I'm not like other people. In any case, he'll be quite independent and I shouldn't mind it if you became his mistress."

Beatrix has gaiety in her eyes. She lies on the bed with one leg raised to deliberately expose her sex. Sabine is annoyed by the way the blonde exhibits herself.

"Well, I'll think about it," Sabine says.

Beatrix laughs.

"It's poetic, isn't it?"

Sabine thinks of the winter in Paris. Then she looks at Beatrix, at the blonde sex, at the pink petals unfurled and waiting.

Such fancies.

Sabine, how wanton, you are.

Chapter Fifteen

*

In 1925 Sabine is having a difficult time again. Daurez has abandoned her and left her nothing. In November it rains every day and Sabine has a cold, a lingering fever that keeps her body flushed and perspiring.

She has a job in a hatbox factory. She works in a large room with twenty other girls. She stands at a long table. Her job is to place the cover on each hatbox as it comes along and then paste the label on the cover. Her eyes are red. She wipes her forehead. She puts the cover and the label on a box and then she pushes the box down to the next girl.

Later, in the office of the boss, Sabine stands against the wall. The small office is cluttered with piled boxes and stacks of paper on the desk in the center of the room.

The boss is a pudgy man, his eyes on Sabine as he touches his moustache.

"I told you the labels need to be exactly in the center."

"I think I have a fever."

"You're saying that because you don't want me to kiss you."

He tries to kiss her anyway. He moves towards her, leans against her and places his lips upon hers. Sabine remains motionless, her back pressed against the wall and her eyes closed.

Sabine's day at the factor finally ends. She blows her nose before she leaves the crowded room. She has a tired walk home, her coat collar pulled up against the light rain that continues to fall on the streets.

The building Sabine lives in is located in a narrow alley. As soon as Sabine passes through the front entrance, the concierge begins shouting at her about the overdue rent. The old woman waves her arms at Sabine.

"What am I supposed to tell the landlord?"

"I'll pay on Friday."

"That's what you said last week. It won't do any more."

Sabine lives in a crowded little room filled with old cartons and dresses and lingerie draped over the chairs. The single window looks out on a cracked brick wall. Sabine sits on the bed. She blows her nose again. She sits alone and miserable as she listens to the rain fall on the grimy window.

*

The next afternoon Sabine approaches a cabaret in Pigalle. The street is deserted except for a man sweeping the sidewalk to collect the debris and empty bottles from the previous evening.

When Sabine enters the cabaret, she finds the place empty, chairs piled on tables, someone in a far corner mopping the floor.

Sabine calls out:

"I want to speak to the manager."

"In the office. Go to the back and you might find him."

In the office the manager is standing near his desk with his head turned to face a calendar on the wall.

"What do you want?"

"I'd like a job."

He looks at her, his eyes roaming over her body. His eyes are dead. Does he have any interest in her?

"What can you do?"

"I don't know. I suppose I can do anything."

"Without experience it's difficult. Can you sing?"

"A little."

He holds a lighted cigarette in his right hand and now he puts the cigarette in his mouth.

"Well, you're pretty enough. Take off your coat."

Sabine removes her coat and she places it on a chair.

The manager nods.

"Show me what you have under the blouse."

Sabine calmly unbuttons her blouse. She strips to the waist, first the blouse and then her brassiere.

The manager reaches out a hand to squeeze one of her breasts. His fingers dig in, his fingertips pushing into the globe of her breast. Then he tweaks the nipple.

"Now the legs. Can you dance?"

Sabine pulls up her skirt to expose her thighs above the tops of her dark stockings. The manager gazes at her legs, at the white skin of her thighs.

"All right, I'll make a spot for you."

Sabine sings on a small stage.

She wears a blue lace affair that falls to mid-thigh but is still high enough to show her garters. She wears red stockings and red shoes and dark red rouge on her cheeks. She sings a song about a girl who is looking for a lost lover.

The room is crowded, filled with people and smoke, bleary-eyed men and an army of whores. The girls are laughing. The two musicians up front look worn out. The drummer has his eyes closed and the man who bangs the old piano stares ahead of him with his mouth hanging open.

Sabine sings. The audience ignores her. She hasn't much of a voice but she sings anyway. When she finishes her song, the drummer opens his eyes to produce a short flourish with his drumsticks. Only a few of the older men in the audience bother to clap as Sabine hurries off the small stage.

Well, the hell with it, Sabine thinks.

She stands with the manager in the dark corridor and the manager purses his lips at her.

"We'll think of something else," the manager says.

He pats her cheek. He winks at her and then he purses his lips again.

Why not? Sabine thinks. One must always be hopeful.

*

Now a few weeks have passed and Sabine has just appeared on the small stage and the audience is shouting its approval at her.

On this night Sabine is dressed like a school-mistress, a prim white blouse, a dark skirt, her face powdered to give her a pale look. She's on the stage with a young man dressed as a school-boy, a young man dressed in a white shirt and a black tie and short schoolboy pants. The young man sits on a bench with his hands folded in his lap and his eyes on Sabine.

Sabine makes a pantomime. She scolds the schoolboy. The audience laughs. The faces of the men are flushed as the whores lean against them.

Sabine begins to take her clothes off.

The drummer and the piano player pound their instruments to add to the general racket.

Applause and catcalls come out of the audience:

"Let's go, let's go!"

Sabine is in no hurry. She slowly removes her clothes, one piece at a time, each piece waved at the crowd before she drops it on the chair beside her.

Before long Sabine is down to her underwear and stockings. The music becomes louder. Sabine turns her back to the audience. She stands with her legs together, her stockings pulled tight by her garters. She slowly unhooks the brassiere, pulls it away from her breasts, slowly turns to face the crowd again.

They whistle at her rouged nipples.

They call out to her. They wave their arms at her. They want the underpants removed.

Sabine obliges them. She drops the satin under-pants and she steps out of them. Now there is only the narrow garter belt that holds up her stockings and an even narrower triangle of white satin to cover her sex. An incomplete covering: Sabine's generous thicket escapes on either side of the white triangle.

The men in the audience call out again, the drum rolls, the piano jumps, the young man dressed as a schoolboy grins at Sabine as she slaps his knees.

Sabine hesitates a moment. Then she turns her back to the audience and she bends forward a bit to emphasize the curve of her bottom.

"Bravo! Bravo!"

They call out to her. The men are shouting and the whores are screeching. They continue calling out to Sabine as she hurries off the stage to the beaded curtain.

*

The First Law of Paris in the year 1925: Without money there is no life.

In the afternoon Sabine is in a shop buying groceries. She buys bread and cheese and she walks out into the street with her arms full. She feels a certain contentment. The sun is shining. She wears no makeup and she likes the feeling of the sun on her face. The man selling vegetables is smiling at her. The vegetable reminds Sabine of the manager Fadeau and now she thinks of her job. Well, it's money, she thinks. The truth is that Fadeau has been kind to her. Oh, he wants her, all right. When he's in the mood for it, she sucks his organ in his office. He calls it playing the flute. Is it time to play the flute, Sabine? He also likes to take her from behind in his office and she can't deny the pleasure he occasionally gives her. She finds a certain excitement in these hurried couplings, Fadeau grunting behind her in his tiny office. He has the other girls when he wants them and Sabine doesn't mind it. What she's not fond of is the sucking. Sabine has no fondness for kneeling on that grimy floor to suck Fadeau until he spends in her mouth. But she does it anyway. And then afterward she goes out on the stage to charm the audience. She makes them quiver. Fadeau stands at the side and he smiles at her as she plays her games on the stage.

It's the money, Sabine thinks. In any case, now she's hungry and she has the smell of the bread in her nose.

*

And then at night it's the crowd in Pigalle again.

This evening after one of her performances Sabine sits at a table with a man and a woman. Friends of the manager. Sabine is relaxed. No need to be on the stage tonight. This couple is pleasant and the manager Fadeau has been kind to Sabine. And in any case it's interesting. Claude and Marie have gracious manners. Sabine smiles. They drink wine together.

Later, in a bedroom on Ile St-Louis, they drink wine again. Three glasses of red wine. They raise their glasses to each other.

Marie undresses as Claude fondles Sabine. A large gilt mirror faces the bed and Sabine gazes at it as Claude kisses her neck, as his hands move down her back and over her bottom.

Claude fondles Sabine's buttocks as his wife continues to undress.

Sabine watches Marie in the mirror. Tomorrow night Sabine will be on the stage again to remove her clothes for the audience. Tonight Sabine watches Marie in the mirror.

Naked at last, Marie holds her small breasts in her hands.

Claude and Marie work together to undress Sabine. Marie fondles Sabine's breasts and then she bends her head to kiss Sabine's nipples.

When Sabine stands naked, the hands of husband and wife move over her body on all sides. Four hands moving, grasping, moving again.

Then three bodies on the bed, the room hot now with human heat and the heat of the fireplace.

The bodies are so pink in the firelight.

Claude takes his wife, Marie's legs over his shoulders while Sabine straddles Maries head to get her sex on Marie's mouth.

Marie's face is hidden.

Claude grunts now as he thrusts into his wife.

Sabine looks at the room, at the elegant furniture, at the gilt frames on the silk-covered walls. She slowly wriggles her sex on Marie's face.

Well, what do you want? Sabine thinks.

Chapter Sixteen

*

In the evening a noisy party is in progress in the salon of the Reina del Pacifico. A phonograph blares out a din of trombones and trumpets. In one corner a number of German passengers are singing loudly with their arms around each other's shoulders.

Sabine enters with Leon. She wears a white dress and white gloves and her emerald necklace. This is the necklace given to her by Leon in Paris and she likes to wear it whenever there is a party in the evening.

As Sabine and Leon walk into the salon, Gustav immediately leaves his friends to approach Sabine and Leon with a smile.

"Ah, it's so wonderful to see you here."

The Germans are singing again.

"What's this all about?" Leon says.

"It's the Rhineland."

"What?"

Gustav beams.

"We're celebrating the remilitarization of the Rhineland. It's time for Germans to stand up for the honor of Germany. We have the right, don't we?"

Leon is suddenly livid, his face flushed to a dark, almost purplish, red color. He turns to Sabine.

"I want to leave."

But Gustav won't have it.

"You must enjoy this occasion with us. It's absolutely necessary that you remain here."

Sabine is bored by it all. Why would anyone want to have a celebration about the Rhineland? Is it the cathedral in Cologne?

"Sit down with me," Sabine says to Leon.

Leon finally obeys her. They sit down at a table, Gustav hovering over Sabine to get her comfortably placed in a chair.

Then Gustav seats himself in a third chair and he shouts to one of the waiters to bring a bottle of champagne.

"You must drink with us," Gustav says to Leon.

"Where's Beatrix?" Sabine says.

"She has a headache."

Leon says nothing. He knows that Gustav is Sabine's lover. What can he do? He sits without saying anything.

So Sabine is between them, Gustav on one side and Leon on the other side. The music goes on, the singing goes on. Gustav puts his arm around Sabine's shoulders, but she pushes him away.

"It's too hot."

Gustav laughs. He's too drunk to be bothered by her annoyance. He continues drinking, his face showing the effects of the alcohol, the pink color gradually deepening to a bright red flush.

And the Germans are singing again. They have their arms raised in a salute of some sort. Gustav begins singing also. He sings louder than the others, his baritone voice booming across the salon.

"He's drunk," Leon says. "It's disgusting."

Gustav continues drinking and singing and waving his arms at his friends across the room.

Finally Leon has enough and he stands up and shouts at Gustav:

"You fool!"

Gustav is suddenly immobilized, one arm raised and his mouth open in the middle of a song. Then he moves, shifts in his chair, pushes the chair back as he tries to stand.

Gustav stands to face Leon.

But in a moment Gustav's eyes roll up and he drops to the floor in a drunken stupor.

The Germans continue singing. The music is even louder now, the trumpets blasting at them as Sabine tries to calm her nerves with another sip of champagne.

*

The next day a great deal of noise can be heard in the cabin Sabine shares with Leon.

He shouts at her. His face is covered with sweat in the tropical morning heat. He waves his arms as he shouts at Sabine.

Then Leon stands near the open porthole with his right hand on his forehead and his eyes wild and darting.

"You want me to die!" he shouts to Sabine.

She stands at the mirror, half-turned toward Leon but her eyes on her image in the mirror. She touches her hairdo with her right hand.

"You're an idiot! I certainly don't want you to die."

"Then why are you leaving? Why! Why are you leaving me for that pig Eis?"

He shouts at her. Everything said again. The words repeated again as the sweat rolls off his forehead.

"I'm not leaving you," Sabine says. "We're still on the ship together. And you'll have Beatrix, won't you? At least until she arranges to have another cabin for herself."

"Dear God."

"Leon, it's time. It's just time for me to move in with Gustav. Be reasonable, darling. You do want to be reasonable, don't you?"

Leon walks over to the bed and he sits down on the edge of the bed with his head in his hands.

"I don't want that German bitch."

"You mustn't feel so bad, Leon. I still love you. And I think Beatrix will be good for you."

"It's a lie."

He wipes his forehead with his hand, his fingers running over his temples to drag the sweat away.

"It's not my fault," Sabine says. "I need to make plans for the future. Don't you see that, darling?"

"But not with Eis!"

Leon's face is flushed again, the wildness in his eyes as he stares at the floor.

Sabine looks at the mirror again.

"Gustav will get a great deal of money from Beatrix. She doesn't want him any more and she'll give a great deal of money to be rid of him."

"I hate them both."

Sabine walks away from the mirror now.

"Leon, you don't understand women."

Leon leans against the wall near the bed. He

closes his eyes and he slowly knocks his head against the wall again and again.

Sabine returns to the mirror to study her face once more.

"Anyway, I'll look after you," Sabine says. "Now come over here and kiss my cheek."

*

Later that afternoon, Sabine has just come out of Gustav's cabin when she encounters Doctor Gordon on the foredeck.

"Look, there's a dolphin," Doctor Gordon says.

Sabine looks at the ocean but she sees nothing. She turns back to Doctor Gordon and she shrugs. Doctor Gordon has an unhappy appearance, his head bent and his hands in his pockets.

"You've moved in with Eis."

Sabine turns away.

"Are you accusing me of something?"

"I don't know."

"What did you expect me to do? I'm free to do whatever I please."

"Yes, of course."

"Leon is very difficult these days."

Doctor Gordon has a sudden hunger in his eyes.

"Come to my cabin."

"That's impossible."

"It's nasty of you to go with that German."

Sabine is annoyed by the bitterness in the doctor's voice.

"Why don't you examine Leon again? He keeps talking about dying and it's horrible. Can't you do something? You're a doctor, aren't you?"

"I think he might be imagining his illness."

Sabine teases him.

"Arthur, don't you like me any more?"

He pulls at her hand and lifts it to his lips.

"I adore you."

Sabine laughs as she pulls her hand away.

She takes his arm. They continue walking until they arrive at the door that leads to the cabins. Sabine holds his arm as they cross the threshold and enter the steaming corridor. She stops. She looks down at the front of his trousers and she sees his erection.

"You're a bad boy."

Doctor Gordon flushes.

"I'm in love with you."

"That's absurd."

"Please, Sabine . . ."

She touches him, her fingertips grazing the front of his tented trousers.

"Arthur, don't be silly."

Now her fingers are more deliberate. She unbuttons his flies and she slips her hand inside the vent to find his organ. She brings out the column of hot flesh in her slender hand.

Doctor Gordon gasps.

"Someone will see us."

"Do you mind?" Sabine says.

Sabine doesn't mind. She works her fingers on his penis, sliding his foreskin back and forth over the plump knob that reminds her so much of a fat cherry.

Doctor Gordon groans.

Sabine carefully finishes the procedure. She

watches his milk splash against the white wall. Not as white as the wall. The drops are clearly visible and in a moment the sperm begins to stream down the wall to the floor of the corridor.

*

Her uncle, wasn't it? It was Sabine's Uncle Hector who taught her these tricks, the hurried fingerings, the palpitating flesh in Sabine's hand, the urging to completion, the mad pushing and pulling to get the serpent to yield its liquid. Sabine remembers her Uncle Hector with his eyes closed. In the beginning Sabine had to be taught everything. She was like a novice who has wandered into a new cathedral. At which altar does one say the prayers, Father? Hector provided complete instruction in the proper position of the hand. Sabine quivered as her fingers felt the delightful throbbing of his flesh, his tumescent stalk. She learned the essentials, the proper tempo, the proper way to squeeze the organ, the proper way to finish her devotions. She remembers her Uncle Hector with his eyes closed and his mouth open. Hector groaning and his organ spurting. One two three four five.

*

Now it is morning in the Eis cabin and Sabine has been living with Gustav for nearly a week. She lies alone on the damp sheets, shifting her body as she slowly awakens, moving her legs and then her arms and then turning her head to the side to stare vacantly at the open porthole.

A sudden knock on the cabin door makes her

turn her head to the opposite side. She's only half-awake; she thinks it's Gustav.

"Yes? Come in."

The door opens. Doctor Gordon slips quietly into the cabin and when he sees Sabine naked on the bed he quickly closes the door behind him.

He stares at her body.

Sabine is annoyed. She covers herself with part of the sheet.

"Well, what is it? What do you want?"

Doctor Gordon looks around at the cabin, his eyes searching as if he expects to find Gustav Eis somewhere.

"There's trouble with Monsieur Mabeuf," Doctor Gordon says.

"Trouble? What trouble?"

Sabine throws the sheet away and she sits up. Now she doesn't care that Doctor Gordon is looking at her. She ignores him as she searches for something to wear.

Doctor Gordon tells her about Leon. He says that Monsieur Mabeuf is refusing to leave his cabin and he's threatening suicide again.

Sabine hurries to get dressed.

"Where's Beatrix?"

Doctor Gordon shrugs.

"Frau Eis seems to have found her own cabin."

Sabine groans.

"She's a bitch, all right. Well, what's wrong with Leon? Are you going to tell me once again that you don't know?"

"I think it's the beginning of paranoia. But no matter what it is, he needs to come out of that cabin. He needs fresh air and some exercise."

Sabine buttons her blouse. She turns away from Doctor Gordon as he stares at her legs. She wiggles her bottom at him as she walks back to the mirror.

"Don't look at me. Turn around while I finish dressing."

Doctor Gordon turns to face the door. Sabine glances at him as she finishes climbing into her skirt.

They leave the cabin together. Sabine thinks about Leon. Why is she so anxious about him? How stupid she is to be so anxious.

When Sabine and the doctor arrive at Leon's cabin, Sabine knocks and then enters the room.

Leon is alone. He looks awful, his face haggard, his hair unkempt.

"Go away."

"Leon, are you going mad?"

"I want to be alone."

"Why did Beatrix leave you?"

"I called her a German whore."

"You're behaving like a fool and you're making all of us miserable. It won't do, Leon. Do you want me to hate you?"

"I won't live with that German bitch."

"Well, you don't have to, darling. But you must come out of this cabin and have some fresh air."

Leon finally agrees. He's quiet now, subdued, his hair brushed back by his hands.

But for how long?

*

Sabine has decided that Beatrix is incapable of love. How silly of that blonde bitch to abandon

Leon. Sabine trembles as she thinks of the first snows of winter in Paris. Can she possibly survive now? There seems to be nothing more for her, nothing more than Gustav and his armbands. She knows about the armbands now. He has three. The colors vary but the motif is always the same: a pair of toothpicks, each toothpick broken in two places and one toothpick placed over the other. When Gustav has enough to drink, he seems quite willing to parade around the cabin with one of the armbands hanging on his organ. Sabine has more than once tickled Gustav to a spurting finish while his penis carries the emblem of his glorious Fuhrer.

In any case, Beatrix is no match for Leon. The blonde would certainly kill him within a short time. They are hardly suitable for each other.

A voice now, a timid cough and Sabine looks up to find Señor Jimenez gazing at her with his dark eyes.

"My darling . . ."

"Yes?"

"Darling, Sabine . . ."

He comes forward. He kneels on the deck and he tries to kiss her as she sits there in her deck chair.

"Not here, you fool!"

Señor Jimenez rises.

"I know all about the German pig. He violates you in my cabin."

Sabine laughs.

"Don't be absurd."

"Sabine, I know everything."

"You confuse me with someone else."

"I beg you, Sabine . . ."

She sends him away. He looks so fragile and wan that she wants to call him back. But she does nothing. She stares at him for a moment, and then she turns to gaze at the sea again.

*

Evening. The moon is glowing on the sea and the passengers of the Reina del Pacifico are thankful for the cool air.

In the Eis cabin Sabine has just crawled onto the bed to kneel with her buttocks in the air. Only a small lamp is lit and the expanse of Sabine's white rump dominates the room.

She's not totally naked. She wears black stockings gartered above her knees and black shoes with high thin heels. She sways her bottom from side to side, a gentle swaying in the cool evening air.

"Go on, do it," Sabine says.

She turns her head to look over her left shoulder.

Gustav is standing a few feet behind Sabine, his gaze fixed on her raised buttocks. He trembles as he looks at her. His face is flushed. He stands fully dressed, but his trousers and underpants are down at his ankles and his organ is thrusting straight out, pink and quivering and in a state of extreme tumescence.

"Sabine, please . . ."

Sabine is annoyed.

"No, I won't allow it. Only your tongue. You can put it anywhere you like, but only your tongue."

Gustav sighs. A shudder passes through him and he moves forward. Because of the trousers at his ankles, he needs to shuffle to make any progress towards her.

Sabine sways her hips as Gustav approaches her.

Finally he's there. His eyes bright, he gazes at her raised rump. Then he makes a low sound in his throat and he bends to push his face against her white bottom.

Sabine wiggles her hips. Her body slowly relaxes.

"There, Gustav, isn't that better? It's much better, isn't it?"

Sabine's eyes are closed.

Gustav mumbles against her flesh. His lips are working, but the sound is no more than a vague mumble in the evening air.

Chapter Seventeen

*

Bernard Jouvet is the first to be denied.

In 1927 Sabine stands on the floor of a place called Le Club Harem. Not Pigalle at all; only a few hundred yards from the Arc de Triomphe and quite elegant. At least the floors and walls are clean and the management considers it necessary to keep a bar stocked with expensive whiskies.

Sabine is veiled from head to toe. A star attraction. The black veils are more or less transparent and one can see that under them she wears only a *cache-sexe*. She holds her breasts in her hands and she pouts at the audience as the five musicians on the stage manage a rhythm approximating an Algerian tune.

She stands motionless now. She has her right leg thrust forward, hands holding her breasts, her buttocks thrust backward to accentuate their curves.

Her feet are bare, nothing but a thin gold chain around her left ankle. Now she raises her right knee until only her pink toes are touching the brown floor.

Behind Sabine, at a small table with a bottle of champagne and a single champagne glass, sits a bald, dignified-looking gentleman whose eyes never waver from Sabine's body.

Sabine is very much aware of the bald gentleman. For the past four nights he's appeared at the same time at the same table and with the same hypnotized look in his eyes.

Another one. She has them rather regularly now, these aging men who seem completely fascinated by her performance, their eyes staring at her as they sit motionless until she finishes her display of artistic talents.

Now the music is calling for Sabine to move again and she once more begins the slow North African dance taught to her by a dark-eyed girl from Oran.

Slow dancing. A sensuous dance plucked out of an Algerian tent. Sabine knows how good she is. She knows how mesmerized the men can be, how mesmerized the bald gentleman is with his champagne that has yet to be touched and his eyes so round as she sways her hips and belly.

Sabine is fond of the Le Club Harem. One of the better nightclubs in Paris. She has something of a name now. She moves her hips to the music and she wonders how many of the patrons are here tonight because of her reputation.

She slides her fingers over her breasts, around each globe and out to each nipple, the points now hard under the flimsy veils.

There are women in the audience, women who stare at Sabine with envy. The men are hungry and the women are envious. Parisians and tourists. Sabine enjoys looking at them; she enjoys the excitement in their eyes.

Before long the moment arrives when the veils are removed. The music is louder now. Sabine's breasts are slowly exposed, her breasts, her belly, her thighs. She moves her shoulders to the rhythm of the music, her belly shaking, her breasts ripe, her nipples like dark thumbs.

Sabine closes her eyes as she moves to the music.

*

The dressing room. Sabine's dressing room is so cluttered this bald gentleman who calls himself Bernard Jouvet looks like a surprised elf in the midst of an arrangement of colorful draperies. He perches on a small stool with his hands folded in his lap. Sabine sits in front of her dressing mirror, her eyes on the mirror as she touches her face.

"I don't know anything about Algeria," Sabine says.

Jouvet has been talking about her dance. His face is flushed. His eyes are glued to Sabine. The little room is too hot and she hasn't bothered to cover herself. She sits there wearing nothing but the *cache-sexe*, her breasts shaking as she raises her right arm to touch her face again.

Oh yes, she knows what it does to him. It's an amusement, isn't it? She doesn't mind it. She deserves to be entertained as much as anyone else. Let him look if he wants; let him look at her naked breasts. She's tired now and her nipples are soft. She's amused because he seems so shy about it. Such a quiet little man with that bald head gleaming like an egg under the harsh light.

Sabine cleans her face. She wipes away the rouge and powder. Jouvet seems overwhelmed by the odor of perfume and feminine sweat.

"Did you hear me?" Sabine says.

Jouvet coughs.

"But the dance is authentic."

Sabine shrugs.

"A friend taught it to me. She's from Oran."

"Ah yes."

Does he care? Sabine glances at the left wing of the mirror and she can see Jouvet still sitting there with that reverent look in his face. It's absurd, she thinks. The man looks completely drugged. Maybe she ought to cover herself, cover her breasts at least. It seems so stupid to cover her breasts now when he's already seen them. And in any case when her nipples are soft her breasts are merely ordinary. The hell with it, if he wants to sit there it's his own affair.

"I'm tired," Sabine says. "After this I'm going home."

Jouvet coughs.

"Won't you dine with me?"

Sabine looks at him.

"Dine? You mean supper? Is that what you want?"

"If you have the time?"

She wants to laugh. But she looks at the mirror instead and she wipes her lips.

"Yes, why not? I suppose I ought to eat something."

She rises from the bench at last. She enjoys his eyes. She enjoys the way he stares at her breasts. She walks behind the screen to dress. Now he's dying out there because he wants to look at her and he can't. She touches her sex. The groove is wet; she's always wet after she does that dance. Maybe that's why she does it. Maybe the audience knows it. Then she thinks of Jouvet again and she decides he must be rich. He has the look of money, that quiet look that comes from a great deal of money in the bank.

She calls out to him:

"Do you live in Paris?"

"Only a few months during the year."

"And where else?"

"In Indochina."

Sabine laughs.

"And do they have clubs like this one in Indochina?"

She comes out now to put on her stockings, a deliberate offering to him as she sits down, as she slips the toes of her right foot into the stocking, as she slowly pulls the stocking up her leg and over her knee to be attached to the long garter.

His eyes never leave her legs as she finishes the attachments.

He's kind, Sabine thinks. She makes a sudden decision that Jouvet has a great kindness in his heart.

"I'm teasing you," Sabine says. "I'm teasing you with my legs."

"Yes."

"I think I like you."

And then she thinks that maybe she's wrong about him. They always want something from her. And the older they are the more they want. All that hungry wanting.

"Come, let's go," Sabine says. "Now I'm ready and I'm starved."

*

He takes her in a taxi to the left bank and they have dinner near the Church of St. Germain. After that she brings him home to the flat near the Luxembourg. She thinks he's quaint now. This bald gentleman who lives nearly all the year in Saigon. Sabine is proud of her little flat. She has some money these days and her rooms in Rue d'Assas are a refuge to her. She likes Jouvet. Now she knows he's a widower. He seems so helpless. She makes him tea and she sits on his lap. He blushes. She opens her blouse and he kisses the hollow between her breasts. She rubs his bald head as she feels his warm breath against her skin.

"You're tickling me."

"I adore you."

"Do you want my breasts?"

She unbuttons her blouse and she slips it off. In a moment the brassiere is gone and her breasts are free. Jouvet fondles each globe with trembling hands. He kisses her nipples, one little kiss on the tip of each point. She wants him to suck. She holds her right breast with her right hand and she feeds the nipple to his lips. She watches his mouth as he sucks at the hard nipple.

"Would you like me to dance for you?"

He slides his hands over her hips and thighs as she rises from his lap. Yes, she wants to dance for him. She feels giddy now, happy at the way he responds to her. It's pleasant in the club, but here the response is more dramatic.

She has a phonograph recording of an Algerian song, something similar to the songs in the club. In a few moments the music is like a warm syrup that flows into the room to heat the blood. Sabine dances, her breasts bare, her belly swaying to the music of Oran.

She drops her clothes as she dances. She teases Jouvet, her fingers working at the buttons and hooks, her legs continually shifting to the rhythms of the music.

Jouvet is mesmerized by the private performance. He keeps his eyes fixed on her swaying belly, his face flushed and his lips moist.

Sabine is amused. At the end she dances for him wearing nothing at all. She dances in front of him, close to his face, her dark nest almost touching his nose.

Jouvet groans as he shoves his face forward to get at her sex.

*

"There's no need to hurry," Sabine says.

She lies on the bed now, stretched out on her back with her arms beneath her head and Jouvet down there sucking at her like a starved puppy.

His mouth is a delight to her, an instrument of intense pleasure. She enjoys the older men because the older men are much better at sucking then the younger men. They approach the meal with more appreciation and they satisfy their appetite with more energy.

Now she teases Jouvet. She pushes him away. She knocks her knee against his bald head.

"Enough," Sabine says with a laugh.

He crawls after her. His hunger is too intense. His eyes are as wild as the eyes of a wild boar.

Sabine laughs and she tells him to undress.

"You can't do much while you're wearing those clothes."

Panting, his eyes red with his craving for her, Jouvet hurries to get naked.

Sabine smiles.

"Do you want to do it to me?"

"I adore you."

He stands naked, his organ extended and quivering, his testicles hanging low in a wrinkled pink sac.

A sudden inspiration takes hold of Sabine.

"I won't let you. You can have anything you want except that. I don't want that ugly thing inside me."

She expects to be amused by his anger, but instead she finds him delighted. He trembles in his delight.

"I still adore you."

Sabine is amazed. Then she finds amusement in it, this need that he has to be denied his pleasure. Or is it more pleasurable to be denied? She remembers hints of it in other men. Is this what they want?

She orders him to suck her again.

"On your knees."

Jouvet shows his obedience as he kneels at the altar. Sabine quivers as she puts her right foot on his head. She pushes at his head. She tingles with a new power. Like a queen, she thinks. She keeps one foot on Jouvet's head as she pulls at one of his ears with her fingers.

"Don't you dare stop until I give you permission."

*

And so it begins.

Two weeks later Sabine is in a chauffeured car with Jouvet. They sit beside each other in the rear of the long car as the chauffeur drives them out to the countryside near Versailles. Sabine is amused by the tall trees, so tall and stately, such dignity in the perfect rows on each side of the road.

And Jouvet has his dignity too. Sabine knows he owns a large plantation in Indochina, but she always thinks of him as a banker. He looks like a banker. Either that or a marquis. Someone dignified and serene.

Jouvet tries to fondle her legs. He slowly runs a hand over her knees, his fingers pulling at the hem of her dress.

Sabine pushes his hands away.

"Bernard, behave yourself."

He trembles. His delight is always intense and obvious when she treats him like a small boy. He quivers each time she demonstrates her power over him. He thrives on it. Her domination puts him in a state of supreme happiness. She adores the power. She adores making him quiver. He's a good sport. He's kind and generous and she never finds any mockery in his eyes. Not like some of the others.

Now she teases him with her legs, her calves, her ankles. He touches her again and once again she pulls away.

"Can't you wait?"

She lifts a hand to his face. She runs her fingers along his pink cheek and up to his bald head.

"Tell me about Indochina," Sabine says.

Jouvet trembles as he begins to speak again. Sabine hardly listens. She looks at the trees, at the occasional farm house hidden by a large hedge. They pass through a small village and for a moment she becomes sad as she thinks of her childhood.

Don't think, little girl. It's always better not to think about anything.

Then finally the car stops and Jouvet announces they've arrived at a place where it might be amusing to walk a bit. The chauffeur doesn't bother to look at them as they climb out of the rear of the car and walk to the woods.

Sabine laughs as she walks with Jouvet. She can't remember the last time she has felt so free. She enters the wood with Jouvet and as soon as they find a tree to hide them, she fondles his organ through his trousers.

"Impatient, aren't you, darling?"

She lifts her dress. She wears no drawers, only the belt to hold up her stockings. Jouvet's eyes gleam as he stares at the dark bush of her sex. He drops to his knees and he extends his tongue to lick at her groove.

Sabine gazes down at the pink tongue that furrows in her sex. She gazes at Jouvet's nose as he sucks at her juices. She moves her hips, pushing at his face with her pelvis. She opens her legs and she squats a bit to get more of her sex on his mouth.

"It's better here, isn't it? Better than at home? Yes, it's much better, isn't it, darling? You're a pig, aren't you? Sucking at me like that. Sucking my little gigi like a hungry pig. Go on, suck it.

You're all wet with it. You're all wet and you adore it."

Yes, he does adore it. He loves it. He hasn't yet done anything else. And she won't allow it. Now she knows that it's better not to allow it.

She trembles now. She hides her trembling as her juices continue flowing. Jouvet is so delighted with her. He continues sucking until she orders him to stop, and then he looks up at her with his bald head and his wet mouth and his eyes so adoring they make her quiver all over again.

*

Towards the end of the summer Sabine sits in a crowded café with Jouvet and she tells him that she won't marry him.

"It's impossible," Sabine says.

The waiters are calling out to each other. It's an afternoon crowd and the petrol fumes from the boulevard are already thick enough to make Sabine's head pound.

Jouvet's eyes show his unhappiness. He wants Sabine to come to Indochina with him. Sabine is calm. She tells him once again that it's impossible. Jouvet mops his face with a white handkerchief and shows his dejection.

"You'll have everything when I die," Jouvet says. "You'll be quite rich."

Sabine is tempted, but she understands the temptation and she pushes it away.

"Darling, it's impossible. I'm a great pleasure for you now precisely because I'm not your wife."

She's fond of him, all right. He's kind. She

doesn't mind his age. But she can't imagine herself anywhere but in Paris. And she would be bad for him. She's too young for a man like Jouvet. What he wants is a constant state of intoxication and sooner or later the intoxication will certainly kill him.

"I can't be your wife. I don't want to be anyone's wife."

Then a few moments later she starts crying. Jouvet is upset and he touches her hand. Sabine quickly regains her composure and she smiles at him.

"You must write to me, Bernard. And whenever you visit Paris I expect you to call on me. Do you promise? Do I have your promise, Bernard?"

She opens her purse now. She extracts a small mirror to look at her face. Then she returns the mirror to the purse and she blows a kiss at Jouvet.

Chapter Eighteen

*

Off the coast of Brittany: May 16, 1936

Dear God, Europe is here; it's in the air and one can see it. Sabine is in a deck chair in the shade, her nose wrinkling at the smell of seaweed and salt. She refuses to follow the example of the other passengers. She abhors the hot sun, even here in the Channel where the chill of the north is already upon them.

Is that bird a sign of something? Sabine watches the gliding of the sea bird, the turning descent, the flutter, the rise again.

Now for some silly reason she remembers the cat that she had when she was a girl, the cat that was killed in the war. She remembers the cat as she found it, the limp body, the presence of death.

I want to have hope for something. I'm not a child any more and I want to have hope for something.

You must have understanding, Sabine thinks. But she doesn't always understand how things happen.

The sea bird again. Or is it another one? Doctor Gordon says they always mean that land is near.

What she wants is to live without harm. And not to be poor. Not a bundle of misery wrapped up in rags and begging for the gift of survival.

She remembers those awful days and nights in Montparnasse. Oh, I don't want that. It's all right for a girl but I'm not a girl any more. She can tell by the way they look at her now that it's not the girlish form they want. She's always a bit surprised by them. These men with a red flame in their eyes. The way the flame grows stronger in the face of denial. Her protection, isn't it? What would she be without it? Like that Italian woman who now once again walks on the deck with her mummy. The same cloche hat, the same long dress. I don't want it, Sabine thinks. I'd rather be dead than wear a hat like that.

She thinks of warm milk gleaming in the sunshine. Her childhood again. She tells herself not to cry. Was she a happy child? But really what does it matter what sort of child she was, the child no longer has any existence. It's not the child who cries, it's the grown Sabine. She cries the tears of uncertainty. She looks at the Italian woman in that horrible cloche hat and she wonders if the woman is certain of anything.

Is Gustav always aware of what he says? How pompous he is. He lifts his chin and he throws his chest out and he squeaks like his little Fuhrer. Dear God, what do they want?

Now Sabine has a sudden memory of her mother in the small square in Vouziers. Sabine remembers the cobblestones. As a child she liked ices, chocolates, sweet things, shouting, laughing and squabbling with her friends. Remembered moments of innocent pleasure. Doctor Gordon reminds her of a boy she once knew in Vouziers. Sabine feels a sudden affection for the English doctor: she likes a man undemonstrative in the company of women. Yes, his narrow face does remind her of that boy.

It's not the same, Sabine thinks. Don't wallow in the past. Don't think about Vouziers or about Paris when you were more capable.

Am I any different now? Of course there's a difference. She's more rounded and fuller in the figure. Not a girl any more. Madame Boulanger. It's a farce isn't it? She knows much more than they think. The young ones are so vain, aren't they? The way Leon always eyed the pretty girls in Santiago.

Are the passengers whispering about her now? Sabine looks at the other passengers on the deck and she imagines them whispering about her. She sees a woman alone, that English Selby woman. Sabine looks at the woman, at her white suit, at her blonde eyes. Sabine imagines the English woman rolling her eyes in her luxuries, the hot flesh throbbing in her luxuries.

Beatrix adores it when Sabine uses her foot. Beatrix closes her eyes and shudders on the floor as Sabine runs her toes in the wet.

And Gustav foams at the mouth in the agony of his enjoyment. The way he groans.

Of course Gustav and Beatrix belong together. They have a sentiment of mutual confidence. Beatrix says all the women in Germany adore Hitler. And Beatrix has such lovely legs, exquisite ankles, the arch of the foot so elegant.

Darling Leon, you mustn't be jealous. The way his cheeks flush.

Does she hate Eis? Sabine thinks of Gustav, of

his pink testicles. She thinks of the way he sweats in that crowded cabin. His tongue is like a serpent in her sex. He wails about Beatrix. The man without clothes is never like the man covered. Gustav's bearing is always so proper, like an upright goat with a stiff spine and a bleating voice. Is it the money? The Eis fortune? Not his fortune, of course; it's the family of Beatrix. Sabine thinks of Gustav as a slave, Gustav naked on his knees, Gustav crawling in the cabin, Gustav giggling when he's told he has permission to laugh. Sometimes he talks about Beatrix with such love in his voice. Sabine thinks of Gustav with his trousers at his ankles. Beatrix does not like to speak of him. She turns away whenever Sabine wants to talk about Gustav. When he feels his pleasure he grunts like a pig. His hands are always so clammy when he touches Sabine's legs. He curses in German. He talks about the Alps. With his mouth against Sabine's sex, he curses his wife's family. Sabine teases him. She asks him about his experiences with French women. Gustav leers as he talks about Paris. He says he doesn't care that Beatrix is a lesbian. What does it matter to him? He sucks hungrily at Sabine's breasts. Does it bother him that Leon is making love to Beatrix? Gustav prattles about the New Germany. Is there a new Germany? Sabine has the feeling it's the old Germany painted brown. She does hate Gustav. She hates Gustav and she pities him. She hates herself more than she hates any of them. Yes, she will go to Germany with them. She will go to Berlin with Gustav and Beatrix. Señor Jimenez has told her the emerald necklace is a fake and she believes him. Leon is such a frightful liar. She has nothing. There is nothing inside her now except a great emptiness, and nothing outside except a black abyss.

Now as Sabine sits there in the deck chair in the shade, a sailor approaches, one of the uniformed sailors who serve the captain.

He salutes Sabine and he hands her a note.

"From the captain, madam."

The captain invites Sabine to the bridge. Sabine is bored and she decides to accept. The sailor blushes when she looks at him. How old is he? Eighteen? What a lovely young stallion he is, snorting at her, sniffing at her, his organ quivering in its readiness for her.

On the bridge the captain pulls at his red moustache.

"I'm delighted you accepted my invitation."

Sabine finds him amusing as he talks to her about the navigation of the ship, his floating kingdom, the dangers of the sea. His eyes remain on her breasts as he talks about the whales in the North Atlantic.

Then the captain makes allusions to the marital problems of certain of the German passengers.

"One gets to know one's passengers. I suppose it's part of the job, isn't it?"

"I don't know."

"You're not with Monsieur Mabeuf now, are you?"

"Is that what you wanted to talk to me about?"

"Is he ill?"

"He complains that he's dying."

Now suddenly the other officers have left the

bridge and Sabine is alone with the captain. Were they sent away? The captain presses against Sabine from behind. She feels his hot breath on her neck. She feels his penis pushing at her buttocks through her dress. She wriggles a moment. Then she laughs as she pulls away from him.

"Don't be silly."

"Come with me to my cabin."

Sabine laughs again as she turns away.

"It's your wife you want, not me."

The captain stares at Sabine with a flushed face.

*

On this last day before the arrival at Cherbourg, a party is announced. A mood of excitement is evident among the passengers. Even Leon seems happy now, his movements brisk and no talk of death as he sniffs the air to catch the smell of Brittany.

A shiver of anticipation runs through Sabine. She thinks of her future and she tells herself it's not necessary to be drowning in pessimism. What she needs is a few years in Berlin with Gustav and the important people he knows. No more than a few years and then she'll make a triumphant return to Paris. She imagines herself as an elderly woman, dignified, comfortable, with glowing white hair and an apartment known to everyone in Paris for its elegance. I'll have one of the most famous drawing rooms. No more dismal relics from the shady past. Nothing but brilliant conversation when you visit the renowned Sabine Boulanger. The maids have all been trained to divine service. Madame Boulanger is a woman of such glorious courage. Look, the windows in the flat are five meters high and the drapes are of the richest velvet.

Sabine imagines herself holding a cat in her arms as she stands at a window overlooking the Seine. The visitors will be announced one after the other by her maid. They will come with devotion and love, young and old, all the famous people of Paris.

Life has certain necessities, Sabine thinks.

And oh dear God, how I want to be in Paris again.

But first Berlin . . .

*

On the evening of the party, the ship's dining room is crowded to capacity. The large room is filled with smoke and noise and the titillation of the impending arrival in Europe. Sabine and Leon and Gustav and Beatrix are dining together as planned.

"I've been reading about the ocean," Gustav says.

He turns his pink face to look at them, to look at Sabine.

Beatrix frowns.

"It's rather late for that."

Beatrix ignores Gustav in order to smile at Sabine. The blonde inclines her head, her blue eyes vacant, her red lips smiling.

A waiter brings another course. Gustav mutters a complaint about the soup. He says he despises thin soup.

Beatrix refuses to talk to Leon. She seems repelled by him. She seems determined to banish all those horrible memories.

Leon has interest only for his food. He munches his bread, sips at his soup, munches his bread again. The hunger never leaves his eyes. He smiles occasionally. He looks at Beatrix, he looks at Sabine, he smiles and returns to his soup.

Then at the far end of the crowded dining room, Señor Jimenez enters. He stands there a moment and he looks around him. His face is haggard, his eyes red. His tie is askew and his left arm appears to be shaking. When he sees Sabine, he gazes at her for a long moment before he finally turns his back to find his table.

Dear God, let it be over, Sabine thinks.

Gustav looks at her and he smiles again.

Sabine shudders. She will go to Berlin with Gustav and Beatrix. They do have boulevards. She asked Gustav and he said yes, they do have boulevards, lovely boulevards that go on and on. Well, it's not Paris, but they do have boulevards . . .

Chapter Nineteen

*

Cherbourg: 4 p.m., May 17, 1936

So now the voyage has ended and Doctor Gordon is standing at the rail of the Reina del Pacifico with his eyes on the harbor and the dock and the soil of France. The sun is hidden somewhere behind a grey blanket of clouds, a dull grey sky and the lights of Cherbourg blinking yellow and the quay already covered by a wet fog. Doctor Gordon straightens up at the rail now. He does not want to be troubled by his imaginings. Sabine is gone, all of them gone, and in a few days he'll be in England again after a month at sea. There now, London isn't Valparaiso, is it? What he remembers now is a brothel near an ugly cathedral, the awful furniture in that large room. The sofa was absurd: twelve or thirteen feet long, red velvet, the back covered with an undulating white lace antimacassar. Above the sofa, on a wall papered with a chaotic arabesque design, a wide mirror with a heavy mahogany frame, a wide strip of glass that showed his face looking back at him, his head tilted, his eyes rather stupid. There were only two women in the room at the time, two women seated on the sofa, one at each end, and both women wore ridiculous pink and white striped stockings, legs striped like peppermint sticks, hair carefully curled and piled up on their heads, antique dresses embellished with a tangle of frills. One woman had a leg up on the sofa, a white shoe with a high heel dangling from her toes, her hand pulling the dress back to show her knee, a red garter at the top of the pink and white striped stocking, the smooth pink skin of her lower thigh. She wore a black shawl and when she turned her head to look at him, she smiled with a broad splitting of her red lips and beckoned to him with her finger.

Sabine, Doctor Gordon thinks. No, it's not possible; that woman was a Chilean whore in Valparaiso. But he has such a fondness for dark-haired women with milk-white skin. He thinks of Sabine and once again he trembles. The breeze blows at his hair. The color of sand, she said. She always said his hair was the color of sand and his eyes the color of a pale blue sky. He remembers her smile, Sabine smiling at him . . .

Nothing now. The drifting fog covers the lights of Cherbourg and the eye sees nothing.

Other Titles Available from Blue Moon

__Beating the Wild Tatoo $5.95
__The Blue Train $5.95
__Bombay Bound $5.95
__The Captive $5.95
__Captive's Journey $5.95
__Elaine Cox $5.95
__English Odyssey $5.95
__Eros: The Meaninng of My Life $7.95
__Excess of Love $6.95
__Fantasy Line $5.95
__Helen and Desire $6.95
__Hidden Gallery $5.95
__La Vie Parisienne $5.95
__Max $6.95
__Mistress of Instruction $5.95
__New Story of O $5.95
__Pleasure Beach $5.95
__Shadow Lane $5.95
__Shadow Lane II $5.95
__The Sign of the Scorpion $7.95
__Beatrice $7.95
__Sabine $7.95
__Suburban Souls $11.95
__Lament $7.95
__Romance of Lust $11.95

At your bookstore, or order from:

Blue Moon Books, Inc.
61 Fourth Avenue
New York, NY 10003

Please mail me the books indicated above. I am enclosing
$_____. Please include $1.50 for the first book, and
$.75 for each additional book, for postage and handling.
Name_____
Address_____
City_____ State_____ Zip_____